Three's Company

It was a bad move. Carter had wrongly assumed that there were only the two of them. He could hear their footsteps moving up on him fast now. He was several blocks from Polteri's building. It was time to brace them.

He ducked into a smaller, darker street, looking for a place to make a stand.

That was his bad move. There was a third. Carter tried to roll out of the way, when he was felled by a tremendous crushing blow on the back of his neck....

NICK CARTER IS IT!

FROM THE NICK CARTER
KILLMASTER SERIES

HELL-BOUND EXPRESS

KILL MASTER

NICK CARTER

JOVE BOOKS, NEW YORK

Dedicated to the men and women of the
Secret Services of the
United States of America

KILLMASTER #256: HELL-BOUND EXPRESS

A Jove Book / published by arrangement with
The Condé Nast Publications, Inc.

PRINTING HISTORY
Jove edition / December 1989

ISBN: 0-515-10199-0

Jove Books are published by The Berkley Publishing Group,
200 Madison Avenue, New York, New York 10016.
The name "JOVE" and the "J" logo
are trademarks belonging to Jove Publications, Inc.

PRINTED IN THE UNITED STATES OF AMERICA

10 9 8 7 6 5 4 3 2 1

ONE

By the time Tony Polteri crossed the Tiber the second time into the Trastevere section of Rome, he was sure he wasn't being followed. Even if he were followed up to that point, losing a tail in the tiny, winding back streets of Trastevere would be simple.

He parked in a narrow alley and walked the few remaining blocks to the square in front of the Church of St. Maria.

Night had descended on the city, but in the narrow streets running off the piazza, streetlamps, neon signs, glaring automobile headlights, and blazing outdoor restaurants frustrated the darkness.

In the middle of all of it, staying in the shadows as he made his way around the piazza, Polteri felt isolated.

He had always felt isolated from what he thought was most people's reality—nine-to-five workdays and clothes for the kids and a mortgaged house in the suburbs and bills for the new car. Polteri existed in a shadow world, with fear his constant companion and himself his only ally. But

1

in an odd way Polteri also felt isolated from this shadow world, aloof from it, as if he didn't really belong, as if he were an observer, not a participant.

He was successful, and because of his success he felt apart. But now the diamond-tough edge of reality was slicing into this illusion, breaking it up. He was a participant, all right. And soon he might die the way many did—in a gutter with a bullet in his brain, alone—not remembered, because he was never really known.

He saw her immediately. Sister Gianna of St. Maria of the Holy Martyrs. She was kneeling in prayer before a statue of the Virgin.

Out of boyhood habit rather than conviction, Polteri crossed himself as he passed through the center aisle and slipped into a pew directly behind her to wait.

Despite the coarse cloth habit and the wimple that covered all but her starkly white face, she was still quite beautiful, with strong Latin features and wide-set dark eyes.

Even after all the years, it was still hard for Polteri to see her as Sister Gianna instead of Joanna Santoni, the prettiest senior at St. Catherine's.

He had been in his first year of law school when they met and fell in love. They couldn't marry; there just wasn't enough money. For two years they suffered, grabbing time together whenever they could. And then the worst thing that could happen, happened. Joanna Santoni, the pride of her family, the most devout girl in her parish, got pregnant. Joanna Santoni, whose two brothers were priests and who, as a child, had thought of becoming a nun, was going to have a child, and she was unmarried.

Her mother had a nervous breakdown. Her two brothers shook their heads, and her father went to the local don in Providence for help in killing Tony Polteri.

Polteri and Joanna bought a simple gold band and, even

though both of them knew the marriage was doomed, eloped. They told no one, and went about their lives as before. The child—a daughter—was born with a defective heart. Joanna named her Antonia, after Tony. The baby lived barely a year.

"It's our punishment, Tony," Joanna had said. "We'll live with it for the rest of our lives."

At the death of their granddaughter, Joanna told her parents about her marriage. Her father pulled strings and obtained an annulment. Joanna Santoni entered a convent and Tony Polteri went to Vietnam.

Suddenly she seemed to sense his presence. She crossed herself and backed away from the Virgin.

"Hello, Tony. It's been months."

"I've been busy." He kissed her on both cheeks.

"Let's go out into the courtyard. I want a cigarette."

"That's permitted?" he asked.

She smiled. "Everything is permitted now, even giving ourselves cancer. You don't look good, Tony."

He shrugged. "I've been under a bit of a strain."

"My brother wrote. He said the flowers on Antonia's grave were beautiful."

Polteri snorted. "With all the money I send that old thief Rosselli, they should be."

They sat on a stone bench that curved around a fountain. He lit two cigarettes and handed her one of them.

"Just like in the movies, huh?" She looked at him and smiled.

"Yeah, kid, here's to you." They both laughed and then fell silent for a moment, Polteri putting his thoughts together. "I'm going to have to go away."

"For long?"

He nodded. "A very long time."

She looked away. "I'll miss our lunches."

He laid his hand on hers where it rested between them on the bench. "Is that all?"

"No. The years have mellowed everything, Tony. We're as close as two friends can be, you know that."

"I know." He withdrew a thick envelope from his inside jacket pocket and set it in her lap.

"What's this?"

"Business."

Her dark eyebrows came together as she hefted the envelope. She didn't know what Tony did. She assumed his business was very successful since over the years he had given nearly a million dollars to her order's children's hospital fund.

"But what should I do with it?"

"Joanna . . ." He paused. It was the first time in years he had called her Joanna.

"Yes?"

"I'm going to write you every month. The letters will come from a lawyer in Geneva. His name and address are there on the envelope. If a month goes by and you don't receive a letter from me, I want you to take that envelope to that lawyer."

Her eyes clouded. "Tony, you're in trouble, aren't you."

He mashed out his cigarette and field-stripped it. "Let's just say I could be."

"Can I help? You've done so much . . ."

"You can help by doing exactly as I say. You will, won't you?"

"Of course I will."

He stood and tugged her to her feet. "I've got to go now."

He kissed her cheek, and then something made him brush his lips over hers. "My God, I'm perverse."

"How so?" she said, smiling, a tear squeezing from the corner of her eye and running down her cheek.

"I always wanted to kiss a nun. Good-bye, Joanna." He moved away, but stopped when she spoke again.

"Tony, when did you make your last confession?"

He paused, then shrugged. "Don't remember."

She moved to him and pressed something into his hand. "Go to confession, Tony," she whispered.

When he turned she was hurrying away across the courtyard, her head bowed.

He opened his hand. She had given him a rosary, and dangling from it, next to the cross, was a plain gold ring.

Polteri's second destination that night—and his last call in Rome—was near the Piazza Venezia. It had once been an elegant old palazzo. Now it looked like a huge pile of dark stone alongside the more modern business district that had grown up around it.

Shunning the ancient elevator that rarely worked, Polteri walked up the five flights of stairs to the top floor. He dropped the brass knocker twice and waited in the drafty hallway, smelling the dampness and the sharp tang of garlic in the air. Light footsteps sounded inside the apartment and the door was opened quickly.

The girl who opened the door looked to be in her middle twenties. She wore a blue denim short-sleeved shirt that was much too big for her everywhere but around the breasts, and a pair of white shorts that appeared to be glued into place. She stood no taller than five two or three, her long black hair tied back into a ponytail that reached down almost to the inside of her knees. Her shapely limbs were tanned to a creamy mocha.

Her face was beautiful. High forehead and straight nose,

the end of which flared into delicately winged nostrils. Jet-black eyes which, round and clear, looked as if they could shift from iceberg cold to sun-hot lava with the snap of a finger. Eyes which, as Polteri made contact with them now, stirred feelings in his groin that he knew he had no business feeling at the present moment.

"Come in quickly," she said in a husky, petulant voice.

Polteri slid through the opening into the foyer of the apartment. She closed and locked the door behind him. "This is foolish, very dangerous," she whispered sharply.

"I know," he replied, "but it couldn't be helped. There was no time to set up a meet anywhere else."

"This way," she said with a sigh.

He followed her into a long salon whose windows looked out onto the elaborate, starkly white war memorial of Victor Emmanuel II. The memorial faced the Piazza Venezia, where Italians had once gathered to hear Mussolini's trumpetings. Beyond it stretched the Roman Forum, and then the incredible bulk of the Coliseum, glowing under its barrage of electric lights.

"Would you like a drink?"

Her nervousness at his being in the flat told him she didn't mean it.

"No, there isn't time. I have a great deal to do. Benjamin Rivkin is going to talk."

Her eyes opened wide and her hand instinctively reached for a cigarette. Polteri lit it and one for himself.

He noticed that his hand holding the lighter trembled slightly. Bad sign.

"How do you know?"

"As investigator of the shuttle ring that brought Rivkin and the other spies in, I was notified. A memo was sent to my office in Vienna this morning. I got it through the office here in Rome."

"How do you know they have turned Rivkin?" she asked, puffing nervously on the cigarette.

"He specifically asked for a top agent familiar with Europe. My guess is he's going to give some of my people—the ones he knows—in exchange for something."

"That's ridiculous. In two, not more than three weeks, Rivkin will be back home, in Russia. The trade is being worked out right now."

Polteri crushed out his cigarette and smiled. "I know. I think that's what he's going to trade for. I think Rivkin wants to stay in the United States."

Her face flushed, as he knew it would. No true Russian and party member wanted to admit that one of his comrades didn't want to return to blessed Mother Russia. She began to pace.

"How did you bring Rivkin in?"

"Vienna, of course. Then he was moved to Madrid, on to Paris, and then through London where he was handed over to your people."

Polteri waited in silence while she paced the floor, lighting one cigarette from the tip of another, and glancing at him every moment or so.

"So Rivkin can name three of your people?"

Polteri nodded. "Rev Babbas in Madrid, Saul Charpek in Paris, and Norman Evron in London. If they get those three, they'll get the other four as well. And, of course, one of the seven will break down and lead them to me."

She stopped her pacing and stared straight into his eyes. "We cannot let that happen."

Tony Polteri stood and strolled across to the terrace that overlooked the heart of ancient Rome. It was beautiful at night, its pillars and broken statuary bathed in spotlights and thrown into pale relief by moonlight.

And the cats. He couldn't see them, of course, but they would be there, hundreds of them prowling for food, moving insolently through the night. Polteri had often gone out and fed them.

He had often fancied himself as one of them.

He would miss Rome, and her. He would miss Vienna and his trips to Budapest and Vela. He would miss Europe, and his women.

Hell, he would even miss the cats.

She was at his side, her fingers on his arm. "Porchov will handle it. He always has."

Polteri shook his head. "Not this time. The agent they're sending to see Rivkin is Nick Carter. He's a bulldog. He won't give up. They were getting close anyway. With Carter on it, it will only be a matter of time."

"No one man can stop an operation as large as this."

"This one can. You don't know Carter. I do." He placed his hands on her shoulders. "We had a good nine-year run. We made one hell of a lot of money. It's over."

"No."

"I'm afraid so," he replied, starting for the door.

"Tony, wait. Let me call Porchov. Talk to him."

"Too late, luv."

"Tony, stop right there."

He turned, and just shook his head when he saw the silenced Beretta in her hand. "I wondered just whose side you would be on when it came down to the nitty-gritty."

"I have no choice."

"Then I'll give you one," Polteri replied. "When I set this whole thing up nine years ago, Porchov insisted on no records, no lists of those I brought across, legal or illegal. I agreed. Well, I lied. There is a master list. Every name is on it. Still think you'll shoot me? I don't think Porchov would like that."

He waited until she lowered the gun to her side, and then threw her a kiss as he went out the door.

TWO

The grilled, narrow windows of the special interview room at Leavenworth let in very little of the Kansas sun.

Nick Carter let his eyes roam around the room without moving his head. There would be a camera somewhere, and at least two microphones. It was common procedure at all federal prisons to photograph and tape any and all interrogations. In the case of a convicted spy like Benjamin Rivkin, it was an absolute must.

But there were reservations about the photos and tapes. AXE chief David Hawk had laid down the ground rules that morning in Washington before Carter had left.

"For now, Nick, your eyes only and your ears only. Confiscate the video and the sound tapes right after you talk to him. MI6 and the Mossad are already aware that Rivkin wants some kind of a deal. If there is any kind of leak, I want to know our trump cards before Israel and our U.K. brethren do."

Carter heard footsteps on the steel plate in the corridor,

and turned toward the door in anticipation. He was looking forward to meeting this man.

Rivkin was a Russian Jew, born in Moscow. Early on, he had been a committed Zionist, speaking out against the Soviet government. He was one of the most outspoken among the refuseniks, and for this had spent a year in the Chistopol prison in the Urals, and another year in a Siberian gulag. Finally he had been retried and exiled into the Jewish refugee program.

What, Carter wondered, had the Kremlin offered him—or threatened him with—that had made him spy for them after he got to the West?

The door opened and Benjamin Rivkin shuffled through. He was a short, gray man, unobtrusive and retiring in nature. He seemed to blend into the room, the city, and the world around him. Only his eyes, alert and speculative, indicated the intelligence behind the monochromatic façade. Now his round face wore an expression of a man who has discovered that the total does not equal the sum of the parts. In his quiet, almost colorless voice, he introduced himself and offered his hand.

"I will not ask for your credentials. I assume you have them or you wouldn't be in here now. And if they were forged and you were an Israeli assassin, I would already be dead."

Carter couldn't suppress a smile. "Shall we get down to business?"

"No," Rivkin said.

"What?"

"I assume this room is wired?"

Carter hesitated and then nodded. "It is."

"Then I insist we talk somewhere else, in the open, the countryside."

"That's highly irregular."

"So is what I have to tell you."

"I could wear a wire," Carter replied.

"You could, but I will search you."

"You're asking for a lot, Rivkin."

"I know."

Carter left him in the interrogation room and went to the warden's office. He made a call to Washington to obtain the proper permission and requisition an unmarked prison van. An hour later they were driving through the rolling farmland of Kansas, with two plainclothes guards in the front seat.

"This looks like a good spot," Carter said, and they stopped.

Carter left his coat and his shoulder holster rig with his 9mm Luger with one of the guards.

"You sure you don't want this?" the guard asked, dumbfounded.

Carter shook his head. "Some farmer might get the wrong idea if he saw it. And, besides, if I can't run a man like Rivkin down, I'd better pack it in."

The guard shrugged. "Up to you. Just remember, if you get out of our sight, he's all your baby."

Carter held his hands straight out from his sides so Rivkin could pat him down. He found nothing.

"You are an honest man, Carter."

"Sometimes," the Killmaster replied, "when it serves my purpose. Shall we walk?"

They climbed over a low chain link fence into a recently plowed field, and began to walk in adjoining furrows. The sky was on fire with a blue brilliance that was almost blinding. There was not a cloud to be seen in the sky.

Rivkin took a deep breath of the crisp, fresh air heavily

laden with the tang of a recent light snowfall. "It is indeed a beautiful country."

"It is," Carter said. "We'd like to keep it that way."

Rivkin chuckled. "I sincerely hope you do, believe me. The bureaucrats are negotiating a trade for me, aren't they?"

Carter nodded. "It's my understanding that they are very near to reaching an agreement."

Rivkin stopped and faced Carter. "I don't want to go back."

Carter kept a straight face. Hawk had already guessed that Rivkin wanted to turn. The question was, did he have anything to offer in return for asylum and a new identity in the United States? Carter asked him as much.

Rivkin sighed. "Truthfully, not enough for a fine house, a car, and sufficient funds to live out my days in luxury. But I don't need that."

"What do you need?" Carter asked.

"A new identity, a social security card, driver's license, a birth certificate, and a few hundred dollars."

"That might be done. Where would you want to go?"

"Eugene, Oregon. I met a woman about a year ago, a Canadian. She owns a small liquor store there. We would like to get married. I can rather fancy myself as a liquor store clerk for the rest of my life. After all, I'm rather an expert on vodka."

"We didn't know about her," Carter said.

"They don't either. I was very careful."

Carter lit a cigarette and broke up a clod of dirt with his toe. "You would be under spot-check surveillance for a year, perhaps two."

"As long as they're discreet."

"You could never get a passport," Carter said, "never leave the country."

"Ah, you think that would be a problem? That's the last thing I would want to do."

"Okay," Carter said, "what have you got?"

Rivkin started walking again. He shoved his hands deeply into his trouser pockets and screwed his face into a mask of concentration. Carter moved beside him in silence. He didn't want to rush the man. Through the interrogation, the trial, and since, Rivkin had said nothing. Absolutely nothing.

Almost anything Carter learned from him now would be useful.

"I'll start when I came over. I suppose your people are wondering how that was accomplished."

"Very much so, especially considering your record as a refusenik and the number of fellow Jews you helped convince the government over there to release."

Suddenly Rivkin laughed aloud. "That is the brilliance, the sheer genius of the entire operation. We Russians have patience. I worked on the cover for six years before I left Russia. As you know, I even spent two years in prison."

"And you were eventually released into the Jewish refugee program. What did they hold over you, Rivkin, or what did they promise you—a Jew—to work for them when you got into the West?"

Rivkin turned and faced him squarely. "Nothing, Carter. They didn't have to. You see, my real name is not Benjamin Rivkin. It's Boris Bablenkov. And I am not a Jew."

Scowling, chewing the butt of an unlit cigar to a shred, David Hawk listened intently as Carter reiterated practically verbatim the Killmaster's interview with Benjamin Rivkin né Boris Bablenkov. A tape recorder in the AXE chief's desk was rolling. The tape would be transcribed the moment the meeting was over, but from the scowl on

Hawk's face Carter knew he would be moving before the last word was put on paper.

At last Carter took a break and Hawk filled the pause with a groan. "So there was a pipeline to get field agents into the States."

Carter nodded. "And into most of the other NATO countries as well. From what Rivkin said, it's so well organized that young Russian agents take years to establish their Jewish backgrounds before coming over."

"Then," Hawk said, "they are built up when they arrive so there will be no hint of anything shady when they take their final post."

Carter nodded. "In Rivkin's case, he was shuttled to this Rev Babbas in Madrid. There, he established himself as a bookkeeper with the Babbas company. After a certain period of time, he accepted a better job offer from one Saul Charpek in Paris. His association with Charpek gave him an in with international banking circles. From there it was on to London, where, with the help of Norman Evron he formed his own investment counseling firm—"

Hawk jumped in. "And then it was an easy matter to make the jump to the United States, where, in the guise of foreign investment in real estate he bought land close to every military installation we have."

"And," Carter added, "built a lot of low-cost housing for military personnel. It's impossible to guess how much information he acquired through the relationships he made."

"My God," Hawk growled, "he could be the tip of the iceberg."

"He probably is," Carter said. "Rivkin believes that it's been going on for nine or ten years. It's hard to say how many agents they have put in place. He only had three names, but he's sure they have at least one man in every country in Europe as part of the chain."

Hawk discarded the soaked cigar and readied another one. "And Rivkin seemed to think that they weren't Moscow controlled?"

"That was the impression he got. It's an independent organization. Moscow foots the bills, of course, and pays well for every agent settled in place."

There was a light rap on the door and Hawk's second-in-command, Ginger Bateman, moved briskly and businesslike into the room. "I've got background on the three of them, but it's short and very sketchy."

"Let's hear it," Hawk said.

"All three of them are refugees. Charpek and Evron came out of Russia, Rev Babbas out of Poland."

"How long ago?" Carter asked.

"Eleven years," Bateman replied. "I ran everything we had on them through the computer. Nothing links them together, even knowing one another. But there is one screaming similarity. Babbas was in the restaurant business in Madrid, and failing. Saul Charpek emigrated to Israel and was eventually asked to leave. Evidently he was a bit of a con man and an embarrassment. Norman Evron owned a small bookmaking operation in Brighton. He got hit pretty hard, couldn't satisfy all his clients, and lost his license. Now comes the similarity. About ten years ago, each of them started his own firm. Rev Babbas in clothing manufacturing, primarily military uniforms. Saul Charpek went into the arms business, and Evron started his investment banking business in London. All of them were heavily capitalized and became quite successful. Since then they have been model citizens."

Hawk and Carter exchanged a long, knowing look. Carter spoke. "Moscow."

"I think we can infer that," Hawk said. "But if Rivkin's right and they are free-lancers, then there must be some control. One person or group of persons is guiding the agents to them for placement and money collection and disbursement."

Bateman jumped back in. "I've instructed our people in London, Paris, and Madrid to dig some more on the three of them. Should I have them put under surveillance?"

"No," Hawk said, "not yet. We don't want to tip them yet. This ring has been on the burner for a couple of years. Didn't the CIA have a man on it?"

Bateman nodded. "Tony Polteri in Vienna. So far, he hasn't come up with anything concrete."

"But he must have something," Hawk said. "Fax what we have to him, and alert him that N3 is on his way. We'll work together on it. All right with you, Nick?"

Carter nodded. "What about Rivkin?"

"I've already got the go-ahead. They'll transfer him tomorrow night. Bateman . . ."

"Yes, sir?"

"Get Nick a flight to Vienna tonight. Also, get a list of every Jewish refugee agency operating in Vienna, even the private ones. None of them may be involved, but they'll have to be checked."

"Right away. Anything else?"

"That's it," Hawk said, and turned to Carter. "Nip this fast, Nick. And get records. If they've been at it nine or ten years, God only knows how many like Rivkin they've put in place."

THREE

The rusted, hand-painted sign illuminated by a bare yellow bulb read Trattoria Bellini. There were several motorbikes and three cars in front when she parked.

Walking from the car to the door, she looked different than she had in the flat with Polteri, more like the streets of Rome. She wore a long black leather coat over a white sweater and loose black skirt. A pair of knee-high black boots completed the costume.

The trattoria was the restaurant, bar, and meeting place for the farmers of the area. A half dozen of them, sturdy, red-faced men in black woollen suits and mud-caked boots, sat at wooden tables with bottles of wine before them, puffing on pipes and listening to a frail, bearded old man who was playing a violin. The room was warm, and smelled of strong tobacco, garlic and stewing tomatoes. It was the natural place to stop for a rest between Florence and Rome. They had used it before to meet.

She spotted Maxim Porchov at a small table along the rear wall. With his wide peasant face, his dark mustache, and his unruly hair, Porchov was not unlike the other men in the room. Only the cut of his suit and the shine on his shoes set him apart.

He stood when she reached the table and kissed both her cheeks. "My dear, ravishing as usual." His Italian was flawless, with a slight Tuscan accent.

"Thank you. You made excellent time."

There was a carafe of wine on the table, and two glasses. He poured. "I flew out of Vienna and drove down from Florence."

To anyone in the place, they would appear to be an old man and his young mistress stealing a short time together. Quite understandable, and commendable in Italy.

She sipped her wine and lowered her voice. "You found him?"

Porchov nodded. "He is in Venice. I have an entire team on him. When the opportunity presents itself, they will pick him up."

"What if he doesn't give you the list?"

The Russian smiled. "My dear, once we have him in a quiet place, we'll get the list, never fear."

"What of the net?"

"It's difficult to say. Of course, the three Rivkin names will have to be eliminated. We are taking pains, of course, to salvage the other four. But the most important thing is to keep the agents we have in place. For that we need Polteri's list. If it should fall into the wrong hands . . ." He shrugged and rolled his eyes toward the ceiling.

"Will there be a problem for you, in Vienna?"

"There could always be a problem. But in the case of Benjamin Rivkin, we might be lucky. He was handed over directly to Rev Babbas and taken to Madrid. It is unlikely that Rivkin even knows of my existence. No, the only person who could harm me is Polteri himself, and that will be taken care of soon."

"What about Rivkin?" she asked. "He is a traitor."

"Our friends in the United States are returning a favor for letting their shipments of precious white powder pass safely through Cambodia and Vietnam. I am sure the quality of their work will be extraordinary, as usual. More wine?"

She shook her head, placing a palm over her glass. "I should continue in Rome?"

"Of course. Your position is far too valuable in many areas. But you could be of some assistance in Paris. Charpek could prove troublesome if he is on guard, and feminine beauty is his weakness."

"I understand," she said with a smile. "I have a small bag in the back of the car."

"Excellent," Porchov said, rubbing his hands together. "Now, shall we dine?"

The train droned north out of Venice into the foothills of the Dolomites. To the right, the ringing blue of the Adriatic became shallow, opague. Along the reef there was a straggle of fishing villages. In their little bays, fishing boats bobbed at anchor, each one decorated on the bow with an eye or a star to ward off evil.

As the train turned inland and began to climb, Tony Polteri gave up trying to see out of the grimy windows and glanced at his watch.

It was six, a half hour before the dining car would open for dinner. He would have just enough time to shave and change his shirt.

He peeled off the shirt he had slept in the night before in the seedy seamen's hotel, and stuffed it into the trash container. Then he lathered his face.

As he began to shave the right side of his face, he went over what he must do in the next few hours. First he would contact Eula Steforski, and tell her that the underground railroad she had been running for so long was over. He owed her that much. After all, without her starting the operation and working so tirelessly for the legitimate part of it, Polteri wouldn't have been able to pull off his end of the operation. And since she had worked so long for little more than expenses, he might even give her a little extra money to relocate. That is, if Maxim Porchov would let her.

The first thing in the morning he would clean out the local bank account and safe-deposit box in Vienna, and then drive over the frontier into Switzerland. Once he had transferred the contents of the Swiss accounts into bearer bonds, he would fly to Uruguay. He already had the go-ahead from General Eduardo Pelodez. Of course, it had cost one million dollars, but that was a small price to pay for a lifetime of safety.

Polteri was just about to shift the razor to the left side of his face, when there was a knock on the compartment door.

"*Sì?*"

"*Pardon, signore.* I have declaration cards for the fron-tier."

Polteri put down the razor and crossed to the door. The lock had barely clicked when it burst open, smashing his forehead. There was a blur of movement and a fist drove into his belly, sending him reeling backward into the bunk.

He gasped for air and opened his eyes.

There were two of them. One was young but bald. He had thick, curly black eyebrows and a hooked nose pitted with oily pores. This one held a silenced automatic, its ugly snout creasing the skin between Polteri's eyes.

Polteri heard a click and rolled his eyes to the second

man. He was even bigger than the first one, with a bull neck and a simian overhang shading vacant black eyes. The blade in his hand was about eight inches long, and he handled it like a street fighter: low, underhanded, the hilt braced against the heel of his hand, the thumb positioned for leverage.

Baldy spoke. "We have come for your list."

"List?" Polteri said, darting his eyes from one man to the other.

"My friend's name is Glenno. He is an expert with the knife, so good he can peel off your skin in layers. The list."

Polteri jerked his elbows upward in a swift, economical thrust. The wrists they struck were rock-hard, but the elbows were harder. There were twin moans of pain and surprise.

Simultaneously, he flicked his foot at the outside of a wrist. The bone-hard edge of the foot grated against Glenno's wristbone. The knife went skittering across the carpet. He stooped to pick it up. Polteri caught him under the chin with his knee.

By that time, Baldy had recovered. He grabbed Polteri's wrist and pulled it toward him. Polteri didn't resist. He pushed in the direction of the pull, adding his strength to the man's. At the point where Baldy's arm wouldn't bend back any further, Polteri put his other hand lightly above the other's elbow. He had the wrist trapped by that time, having whipped a big hand around in an acrobat's grip. Baldy's arm broke at the elbow with a sharp crack.

He screamed. Polteri kicked him in the crotch. Baldy fell to the floor in agony, and Polteri spun to locate Glenno, the knife wielder.

Glenno's blade had sailed under the bunk, but he had

grabbed Baldy's heavy automatic by the silencer and was swinging it with all his might.

There was no way Polteri could avoid the blow. It hit him in the center of the forehead and he dropped like a rock.

Glenno turned to his comrade. "Pietro, are you all right?"

"Bastard, he broke my arm! And, oh God, my balls . . ."

Glenno was not the brains of the pair. For a full five minutes he knelt helpless on his knees by his friend waiting to be told what to do.

Finally Pietro was able to speak. "Water, get me some water."

The hulk moved to the basin and came back with a paper cup of water. Pietro drank it greedily and handed it back.

"Fill it again and throw it in the bastard's face. Wake him up!"

"*Sì, Pietro, sì.*"

Glenno did what he was told. When that didn't work, he did it two more times. When he started slapping Polteri's face and still nothing happened, it began to dawn on him.

"Pietro . . ."

"What?"

"I think I hit him too hard."

"What did you say?"

"I think he's dead." Glenno crossed himself.

Pietro crawled to Polteri and checked his pulse. "*Idiota! Stupido!*"

"Pietro, I-I'm sorry . . ."

"Shut up, let me think!"

Pietro thought quickly, forcing the pain out of his mind. There would be hell to pay for this. The best thing would be to make it an accident, he thought. But in the meantime . . .

"Glenno, help me search . . . everything, his clothes, his wallet, the compartment . . ."

"*Sì, sì.*"

"Look for a list of names, or maybe a code list of numbers."

They took the bag, the wallet, the clothes, and the compartment apart. They wrote down everything that looked like a list or had been written in Polteri's hand. Then they put everything back just the way they found it.

"Now we dress him."

"What for?"

"Because he's going to have an accident. He's going to fall off the train."

FOUR

According to his ticket, Carter had fifty-five minutes at Heathrow to catch his British Airways connection to Vienna. He need not have worried. BA flight 729 was three hours late taking off.

To make matters worse, economy class on the flight was completely booked. The only seat Ginger Bateman had been able to get him was in first class. He would have preferred one of the cheaper seats: economy class was anonymous. First class passengers were much more conspicuous, particularly on smaller aircraft.

Eight passengers besides Carter sat forward of the pleated partition, separated from the common herd. One was a handsome, high-nosed, querulous old lady surrounded by an aura of wealth who traveled with an animal of some kind in a pet carrier she kept on the seat at her side. The box whined from time to time and was comforted, or had its wishes relayed to a stewardess by its owner in a clipped British voice that commanded attention.

Two others were Japanese, an unobtrusive middle-aged

couple who said "Prease" and "Sank you" to the stewardess when she paid them any attention. Another, younger couple, Americans, were newlyweds by the look of things; in love, they drowned in each other's eyes, oblivious of what went on around them. They traveled on a pink cloud of their own, cut off from the world.

The last pair was an odd couple, two men who were obviously not traveling together. One of them was a very large man, inches over six feet and wide in proportion, not fat, but huge, and loud. He was also very drunk. His seatmate was a small, dark man with a neatly trimmed mustache who was obviously uncomfortable.

The seat beside Carter was empty, but not for long. When they had reached cruising altitude, the dark little man stood and moved back to Carter.

"Excuse me . . ."

"Yes?"

"I hope you won't mind, but I wonder if I might change seats. I am really not equipped to ride for several hours in the company of that buffoon."

Carter smiled. "Sure, sit down."

"Thank you, thank you very much." The man slid into the seat and offered his hand. "Justin Feinberg. I'm Israeli."

"Nick Carter, American."

The two very blond and very pretty flight attendants began to serve lunch. Five minutes into it, Justin Feinberg started to chatter.

"I lived in New York for years. Did a lot of business with Tel Aviv. I was gone so much my wife suggested we move there."

"Is that right?" Carter said, forcing down some wilted lettuce.

"I'm in farm machinery. You?"

"Government," Carter said, "State Department. I shuffle papers."

Two more bites and coffee to kill the taste.

"I'm staying at the Imperial," Feinberg said. "Always stay at the Imperial when I'm in Vienna. You?"

Carter's antennae were starting up. "I didn't make reservations. It was a short-notice trip."

"Really? That could be a disaster this time of year. Wagner lived there, you know, at the Imperial, so he could be near the opera."

"I didn't know that." Carter pushed the meal away and concentrated on the coffee.

"Give me a ring there if you can't find anything. I've an in with the concierge."

"I'll do that."

Feinberg kept up that chatter until the food trays were taken away, and then excused himself. The man could be harmless, just making conversation with a fellow traveler. But the questions were a little too pointed.

Carter hit the rest rooms and then darted into the forward galley where the prettier of the two blondes was doing a quick cleanup. It was she who had taken his briefcase containing his 9mm Luger, some spare clips and the stiletto he affectionately called Hugo. The way she had written out the receipt told him that she was not a little thrilled by big bad men who ran around the world with guns.

"Excuse me . . ."

"Yes, Mr. Carter?"

"You've already seen my credentials."

"Oh, yes, sir."

"I wonder if you would do me a favor."

"I can try."

"My new seatmate. Do you have his name and nationality?"

She reached for a clipboard hanging behind her and a
carefully manicured nail went down the passenger list.
"Mr. Justin Feinberg. He's an Israeli."

"And the slightly inebriated gentleman in the front seat
where Feinberg was sitting originally?"

She went back to the list. "Aaron Horowitz."

"And his passport?"

"He's also an Israeli."

Some pressure on Carter's side brought him out of his
nap, and as he tried to ease this pressure he realized that
someone was nudging him gently. The smiling face of Justin Feinberg was bent toward him when he opened his
eyes, and as he sat up and started to yawn his companion
gestured to the lighted sign that instructed the passengers to
fasten their seat belts.

"Oh. Thanks."

"It seemed best to wake you," Feinberg said. "You had
a good nap."

"I guess I must have," Carter grunted.

"Perhaps we could share a cab into the city together?"

"I don't think so," Carter said. "I have someone meeting me."

Conversation ceased as the plane touched down and
taxied toward the terminal. As soon as the jetway was attached, the line of people that had squeezed into the aisle
surged forward, Feinberg among them.

Carter smiled. Whoever the man was, he wanted to
make sure he and his hefty pal got in place for a tail before
Carter got through Customs and Immigration.

Near the tail end of the line, Carter stood and moved
along the aisle. The blonde had his briefcase ready. He

went through VIP customs, and found Hans Meyer waiting for him.

Meyer was a bandy-legged man with a thick, powerful torso that didn't match the legs. His arms were posts and his head was neckless sitting right on his shoulders.

His cover was as a driver for the American embassy in Vienna. As such, he was in a perfect position to keep score on all sides of the game.

"Herr Nick, good to see you."

"Hans, a long time. Where's the car?"

"Aisle four, blue section, three cars in. It's a blue Opel."

"Got a camera in it?"

"Always."

"Get it. I want a shot of the little one over there with the mustache. Also whoever he teams up with."

"You got it. I'll meet you at the car."

Meyer scooted away. As soon as Carter got his bag, he took a long walk through the airport and found the car. He tossed his bag in the rear and sat smoking until Meyer arrived fifteen minutes later.

"The little guy made contact with a tall, skinny guy in a Citroën. You had a big chunky one trailing you through the airport to the car. Then he joined the other two in the Citroën."

"You get the pictures?" Carter asked.

Meyer tapped the Nikon hanging around his neck. "All three are down for posterity."

"Let's go."

Meyer crawled in and drove like the native he was from the parking lot, honking everybody out of the way.

"Have you been briefed?" Carter asked.

Meyer nodded. "Bateman gave it to me on the scrambler phone last night."

"What about Polteri?"

"Checked his office this morning. He was due in yesterday morning from Rome. He's not there yet. Secretary says not to worry, he does it all the time. Where to first?"

"Bonlavik still around?"

"Oh, yeah, same stomping grounds. But he's not very active anymore. Hell, the guy must be close to eighty."

"All of that," Carter said, "but he's a walking encyclopedia on everyone coming over and how they made it for the last twenty-five years."

"He is that," Meyer agreed, nodding. "You want to hunt him up?"

"Yeah, but just drop me inside the Ring. I'll walk. You get rid of my bag and get that film developed. When you do, run it through Washington with the names Justin Feinberg and Aaron Horowitz."

"Israelis?"

Carter nodded. "Hit our Mossad file. My guess is that's where you'll find 'em."

"What do we do about them now?" Carter turned the rearview mirror his way. "Six cars back," Meyer said, "not pushing it, just keeping their distance."

Carter spotted the Citroën in the mirror. "Got 'em. Where have you got me staying?"

"Pension Poston, inside the Ring on Ulborstrasse. The room number is seven. Here's the key."

"Okay. Take the Ringstrasse to the opera house and hit that alley that leads around behind the Bristol."

Meyer smiled. "I know it."

"I'll dive out there, see Bonlavik, and meet you at the pension in a couple of hours."

"*Ja, ja, mein Herr*, and away we go!"

Meyer tromped it and the little Opel leaped ahead.

Traffic increased as they entered the city, leaving the

highway to roll down cobbled streets between gray stone buildings that stretched in rows like parallel walls. The ornate façades of equal height were broken from time to time by domes atop circular corner turrets, chimneys, and occasional mansard roofs.

At the Danube Meyer swung back onto the Ringstrasse and really floored the little car. They darted like a blue gnat in the heavy traffic, and by the time they reached the opera house, Meyer had a full block on the Citroën.

The tires screamed as he hit the alley and turned in behind the opera house. A hundred yards farther on, he hit another right and then an immediate left, which brought them through the maze of alleys to the rear of the Bristol Hotel.

Directly across from the rear of the stately old hotel was the parking garage. Behind its entrance were four huge garbage dumpsters.

Meyer didn't stop at the dumpsters, he just slowed.

"See you," Carter said, and rolled out of the car. He kept rolling right between two of the dumpsters and sat, leaning against the wall.

He counted twenty before the Citroën screamed by, then lit a cigarette and strolled across the alley into the rear of the Bristol. He went on through the lobby to the cabstand in front of the hotel.

"The Tuchlauben," Carter told the driver, "no hurry."

Carter's destination was an auto repair garage on a cobbled street about two blocks from the Danube. By the time he reached it, the temperature had dropped considerably and there was the feel of snow in the air.

It was an old cement-block building, with a roll-up door barely wide enough to admit an automobile. There was a street door next to that one, and above him, on the second—the top—story, were three paint-blackened windows with wire grilles. There were no signs in front and no lights glowing inside or anywhere else along the street. In the rear there were rickety wooden stairs leading to the second floor. Carter took them.

He hadn't seen Emil Bonlavik for nearly five years, but he knew the old man would help him.

In the old days, before and during the Nazi occupation of Hungary, Bonlavik had been a resistance fighter and a Communist organizer. Then, after the Reds took over after the war, he had broken with them. He had faced the bitter truth that he had squandered years of energy and devotion in a cause rigged by power-hungry mini-dictators.

But he had stayed in Hungary to help others escape. Then, when it became too hot over there, he himself had escaped and continued to help others flee to the West.

About five years ago, he had tried his last coup, and failed. Riddled with bullets and nearly dead, Carter had gotten him out.

Carter rapped on the door at the top of the stairs, and a series of coughs that became words answered him.

"Who is it?" a voice asked in German.

"An old friend."

"I have no friends."

"Nick Carter."

The door opened.

Emil Bonlavik had aged, but in spite of it he was still upright and slender. His hair was still full but it was snow-white now, as was the spade-shaped beard. The contrast to his dark, weatherbeaten face made him seem still strong and decisive. But there was no strength in his gray, short-sighted eyes, only a weak bewilderment and amiability.

"I do believe it is you."

"It is," Carter replied.

"I suppose I'm glad to see you. Come in."

Carter hid his surprise and followed the old man into the room. It was small, cluttered with manuscripts, books, and correspondence. The scant furniture was threadbare. A coal fire glowed hotly in a grate.

Bonlavik slumped into a deep chair. "A long time."

Carter nodded. "Five years."

"After so long a time you come to see me? It must be business. I am retired."

"I know," Carter said, producing a bottle of slivovitz. "I've come to pick your brains."

"My brain has withered with age. There is a glass there. None for me. My stomach."

Carter took his time getting the glass. Something foul was eating the old man. This was far from the greeting he had expected. He poured, slipped out of his coat, and took a hard-backed chair across from Bonlavik.

"Emil, I thought we were friends." The thin shoulders shrugged. "You want to tell me something?" Carter asked.

Bonlavik thought it over and then leaned forward with his elbows on his knees. "We were betrayed that night."

Carter downed a good swallow of his drink and nodded. "I know."

"But do you know who betrayed us?"

"No."

"One of yours."

"What?" Carter said, his spine tightening up.

"It is true. One of your people passed the word. That was how they knew the time and the place where we would be crossing."

"Who?"

Bonlavik sighed and slumped back in his chair. "That I do not know. For a couple of years I tried to find out. Nothing, except whispers. And do you know what the whispers were, all of them? 'The American.' That's all I ever heard, 'the American.' Do you remember Erik Slavitz?"

"Yes."

"And the Krauses, Helga and Stern?"

"I remember," Carter said. "They were my contacts once."

"Killed, murdered, and their bodies never found. Do you know why? Because 'the American' wanted the business."

"Business?" Carter exclaimed. "It was never a business, bringing people out!"

Bonlavik cackled with scorn. "It is now. When Slavitz and the Krauses were killed, word filtered back to me: stop asking questions or I would be next. I quit and became a hermit. The hell with you all."

Carter sighed and returned to the bottle. "Emil, I need your help."

"I can't help anyone anymore. I have become a coward."

"Emil, someone is smuggling Jewish refugees out. One out of every ten or so is a phony, a Russian spy. They are placing them in the West, and doing a damn good job of it."

The old man's eyes came alive for a moment. "How long?"

Carter shrugged. "Don't know, could be years."

"The American," he mumbled.

Carter knelt by the old man's chair. "Emil, if it is an American, I want him. You know everybody here and over there who is moving people. Here's a list. Is it complete?"

For a few seconds Bonlavik shied away from the paper. Then his old curiosity took over and he snatched it from Carter's hand. Quickly he scanned it, and then went back over it slowly, pointing at names with a bony finger as he spoke.

"Dead . . . dead . . . no longer in Vienna . . . dead . . . in prison . . . working through Prague now . . ."

Carter listened until the end of the page was reached. By then a pattern seemed to be establishing itself. "Is that all?"

"All that I know about. There could be others. Some on this list are still operating in a small way. None on the level you're talking about."

"Could you find out?" Carter asked.

Another sigh and Bonlavik closed his eyes. "You ask a lot, my friend."

"I know, but it could be the most important thing you've ever accomplished, Emil. There must be some record of who they have brought over, a list of names. If we can get that list . . ."

The old, watery eyes opened and turned on Carter. "And the American? Would you go after the American who betrayed us?"

Carter nodded. "If there is one."

"Oh, there is one, my friend, I assure you. All right, I'll see what I can do."

The Killmaster looked around the shabby quarters. From a roll in his pocket he peeled off several bills and placed them on the table near the door.

"Expenses."

The old man said nothing. He didn't even look up as Carter left.

The pension was ancient, deep inside the Ring. It had once been a rich merchant's town house that now had been cut up into separate rooms.

Carter entered the reception area, a small affair with

dim lights and stiff, brocade-covered chairs. In the gloom he saw the dark wood of the reception desk. Behind it was a small, prissy man wearing wire-rimmed glasses.

He looked up with a frown and Carter let the key swing from one finger as he headed for the stairs. The man said and did nothing. It was a good bet the pension was used quite often by Hans Meyer for just this sort of thing.

The room was old-world, high-ceilinged and comfortable, with a private bath. His bag and briefcase were on the bed.

He looked longingly at the big quilt-covered bed, and forced himself to strip and head for the shower. A half hour later, shaved, showered, and fifty percent refreshed, he was buttoning a clean shirt, when there was a knock on the door.

"Yes?"

"It's me."

Carter opened the door a crack and Hans Meyer's bulk slipped into the room. He looked around, spotted the flask Carter always carried sitting on the dresser, and headed for it.

The Killmaster threaded a tie through his collar. "What have you got?"

"Their passports are legit, but Justin Feinberg and Aaron Horowitz aren't listed in our files as Mossad agents or operatives."

"They could be part-timers," Carter offered.

Meyer downed his two fingers of scotch and poured another. "They could be, but I doubt it. If our Israeli comrades were going to put someone on you, they would send seasoned pros. They know you."

"Good point. What else?"

"The third man, the hulk driving the Citroën . . ."

"Yeah?"

"Name's Otto Franz. He's an East German, slipped into the West about four years ago. His passport was revoked about a year ago. Interpol has a want on him for questioning in a double homicide."

Carter pulled the knot of his tie tight and turned from the mirror. "An East German involved in a double murder and two Israeli Jews. That's an interesting combination."

"*Ja*, isn't it," Meyer said dryly.

Carter sensed that there was more. "You've got that look, Hans."

"Call it disgust."

"Lay it on me," Carter replied.

"Word came into the embassy from a police prefect up in the mountains about an hour ago. Tony Polteri. He fell off a train just the other side of the Italian frontier and brained himself."

Carter's lips set in a thin line. "Sure he did."

FIVE

The bar of the Paris Lotti was cozy, with a high ceiling and muted lighting. It was paneled in dark polished wood, and the floor was wood of the same color. Oriental rugs were scattered about, and the chairs, arranged around low tables, were upholstered in soft colors.

Saul Charpek strolled casually into the bar, glanced around, and moved toward a stool at the far end away from the door. He ordered an American-style martini, drank it quickly, and ordered another.

Even at a casual glance Saul Charpek was the kind of man people noticed immediately and said nice things about. He was tall, extremely handsome, with clear brown eyes, a strong jaw, and wavy black hair curling over his collar. Combine his looks with a conservative taste in clothes, a well-modulated, cultured voice, and here was the perfect picture of the successful cosmopolitan man.

But as of four o'clock that afternoon, he was no longer Saul Charpek. He had registered at the Lotti with a passport bearing an Italian name and an address in Caracas.

The thought of it made him ill. The false passport and
other papers had been obtained years before in case the
operation ended. In that time he had invested money and
bought property in Venezuela for the day he might need
them.

He had returned to his office that afternoon from a long,
very profitable business luncheon, to find the letter. The
return postmark read Venice, which meant nothing. The
Personal—Urgent scrawled across the bottom of the envelope meant a great deal, as had the sheet of paper with the
words, *ALL IS LOST.*

They said it all. Polteri had said that one day it might
come, and Charpek had, for years, scanned each day's mail
with trepidation. But when it never did come for so long,
he had almost forgotten about it.

Then it had come, the code words that meant the gravy
train was over: run, lose yourself, hide and stay alive.

He hadn't even returned to his flat. He had gone directly
to his bank and withdrawn all but a few hundred francs
from his running account and gotten the false papers from
his safe-deposit box. Then he had bought a bag and filled it
with enough clothes and accessories for the trip, and
checked into the Hotel Lotti.

He was booked on a 7:40 flight in the morning.

Charpek sighed and looked around the room. He would
miss Paris, the food, the ambience, the theater, the women
—most of all the beautiful, chic Parisian women. He
would miss them most of all.

His thoughts were interrupted by the arrival of a new
girl, dark and long-limbed, dressed in a tightly belted
trench coat that emphasized her fine legs and narrow waist.
She had very nice eyes, and a wide smile that she lavished
upon him as she passed. He smiled back, let his eyes flick

quickly over her body, and observed that she was alone. That was significant.

Should he make a move, ask her to join him for a drink? It would be a disgrace to spend his last night in Paris in a lonely bed.

She shrugged out of the trenchcoat. Beneath it she wore a low-cut black cocktail dress that molded her full breasts. Her drink came. As she sipped it, their eyes met again. They were gentle, friendly, sensual.

He looked around. She seemed to be alone—what tremendous luck. Or was it? Another trap? He squinted at her critically. If this was a trap, he could have a hell of a lot of fun falling into it.

He waited until her glass was nearly empty before moving down the bar. "May I buy you a drink?"

Her smile was demure. "You are very kind."

He ordered for her, and they left the bar for a corner table, with high-backed leather chairs. Her dress rustled as she walked, and a slit up the side gave a glimpse of a sleek thigh.

When they were seated, she gave him a beautiful smile. She was a very feminine girl. Her eyes were large, and very brown; her lips were large, her teeth even and brilliantly white. Her face was a perfect oval, framed by very long, jet-black hair.

Charpek introduced himself with his new name and told her he was an attorney, in Paris for just the night. She said she was an airline stewardess with a one-night layover. It was a pointed reply, and Charpek turned on all his charm as he raised his glass in a toast.

A half hour later they moved toward the lobby. There was a large blond man seated by the elevators. For a brief instant Charpek met his eyes, and then the big man looked away.

It was slightly unnerving, that exchange of glances, but the woman was willing on his arm, soft and warm, and his thoughts were elsewhere.

"I have some brandy. Would you like a nightcap?"

"That would be nice," she replied, dropping her coat across a chair and moving to the door that connected his room to the one next door.

"What are you doing?"

"An old habit," she said with a little laugh. "Just checking to make sure the door is locked. I don't like to be disturbed."

She perched on the side of the bed as he handed her the snifter of brandy. Sipping at the heady liquid, she leaned back on one elbow. The gown parted at the neckline. He saw the rise of one creamy breast, round and full at the end.

"I like a man who comes immediately to the point," she murmured.

"Do you?" he said, setting his glass aside and following the slit of her skirt with his finger. "With only one night it would be silly for us to engage in subtleties."

"I quite agree."

She sat up, moved toward him, and her eyes turned to fire as her lips came against his mouth, warm, soft. He felt her press against him, her tongue moving out with quick, darting invitation, then suddenly drawing back. She paused, then moved from him. In her eyes was no amusement, no cool toying appraisal, only a dark, deep hunger.

He reached out, into the neck of the gown, his fingers moving across her left breast, feeling the soft warmth. The gown parted, a small zippered opening becoming wider, deeper.

His hands reached up to pull the gown away from her,

and he felt her tremble under his touch. Her breasts came out of the gown, pear-shaped, pink tips standing out sharply, anticipatory. Her arms encircled his neck, pulling him forward, his face into her breasts. His mouth found the erect pink-brown tips, drew on them.

"Oh, God, oh, oh, please, please," he heard her murmur, and in the murmur there was urgency, a whispered fierceness.

His mouth stayed on her breasts, moving from one to the other, pulling on them, drawing their creamy softness up. She writhed under him, the dress disappearing. Her hands pulled at his trousers, pushing them down to the floor. She pulled him onto her, rubbing her soft belly against him, reveling in the touch of flesh against flesh.

He felt the clawing heat of her body as her leg moved over his and her hand drifted down his stomach.

Then she rolled on top of him. She put her mouth over his and moaned into it. The noise she made was loud and artificial, and it sent a warning through him like an electric shock. Above the sound of her moan he heard the click of the door, and he knew he had been betrayed.

He lurched up from the waist, trying to push her off. But her arms slipped around him and locked behind him. Her legs were intertwined with his, pinning him to the bed. He thrashed to the left, then to the right, but she held him as though her life depended on it.

He looked beyond her disheveled hair and saw two men slipping around the edge of the half-opened door as silently as shadows.

He rolled himself, with her still holding him, to his left, and then off the bed. He landed on top of her and she gasped, stunned, her arms falling away from him. He reached up to the night table, but her hands clawed crazily at his arm, hampering it. At last his fingers curled around the back edge of the dresser.

At that moment he felt a jarring kick on his arm that left it numb. Then the muzzle of a gun was pressed deep into the back of his neck, pushing his face into the carpet.

A voice, cool and calm, said, "Freeze. It's all over."

He lay motionless on the woman, his breath rasping into her hair. His hand slid down the leg of the night table, empty.

"Yes," he said. "It's all over."

Dressed, the woman strolled casually out the front door of the hotel.

They took Charpek out the rear exit into an alley. There he was shoved roughly into a battered old Renault. The half-full bottle of brandy was shoved into his hands.

"Drink it," the big blond man said. "All of it."

The old woman lived on Rue Lepont. It was a dark street that ran above the cemetery in Montmartre. She was only a block from her flat when she saw the two drunks staggering on the opposite side of the street.

Later, she told the police that the car was dark. It was old and battered, but she didn't know the make or model. She knew very little about cars, and besides, all she could really remember was the man's broken, twisted body flying past her as she screamed.

The dead man was listed in the morgue from the name on his passport. A telegram was sent to the Caracas address, but no reply was ever received.

An autopsy revealed the man was very drunk when he staggered in front of the car.

It was listed as a hit and run. The case was closed.

• • •

Madrid's Plaza de Toros was full, even on the sunny side. A low buzz of anticipation came from the huge crowd as the matador strutted toward the bull, his long, curved sword holding the *muleta* out to his right side.

The youth sitting in his shirt-sleeves did not buzz with the crowd. His eyes, which were black and very bright and intense, were fixed on the couple in the box just across the aisle below him.

The man was of medium height and squat figure, dark-skinned, heavy-featured, with small brown eyes set under heavy brows. His clothes were expensive and conservative; a dark blue suit, a white shirt, and a striped tie.

His name was Rev Babbas, and besides owning the gigantic company that manufactured all the uniforms for the Spanish military, he sponsored young bullfighters. It was his hobby and he loved it.

The woman beside him was his current mistress, Estrella Diego. She had been a dancer until she took up with Babbas. She was not a beautiful woman. Her face was plain, square, brown, with a rather wide short nose, wide mouth with a heavy lower lip, heavy eyebrows that she did not pluck, and large shining brown eyes. Her hair was black, parted in the center and curled down over the nape of her neck.

It was her body, however, that caught the eye and, having caught it, held it. It was rich and full like a grape at harvest time. The blood seemed to push against the smooth browned skin, stretching it taut like a full wineskin. She was wearing a simple black dress whose wide vee neckline was cut down from almost bare shoulders to the deep hollow between her breasts. Her arms were bare, browned, and round.

Now and then she would turn sideways to speak to Babbas. When she did, the young man above and behind her could see far down the deep front of her dress. His thin lips parted in a cold smile, startling in one so young.

The man and woman were seated directly over the *callejon*, the narrow passageway between the grandstand and the *barrera*, where the bullfighters stood waiting their turn at the bull. As the young man toyed with a large amethyst ring on his left hand, he gauged the distance from Rev Babbas to the next aisle.

As the matador passed the bull with a swirl of the rose-colored cape, the crowd roared *olé* in time with his movements, the *o-* long and drawn out, beginning as the matador started his pass with the cape, and the *-lé*, more staccato and crescendo, punctuating the maneuver. Four times the matador passed the black bull, alternating from left to right. But the young man did not join in the *olés*. He was waiting for the next charge and for the matador to take the bull.

In the ring the matador swung out the scarlet cloth and steadied the sword over his left arm. The man's body was ramrod straight, his arms stiff, as he watched the bull gather itself, pull its forefeet together and lift its tassled tail.

A hush fell over the crowd.

Then the head lowered and the bull charged, its hooves making thunder on the gray-tan sand of the arena.

The kill was swift, clean, the sword entering to the hilt. The bull staggered twice and toppled.

The trumpets blared and the orchestra took up the theme. The entire bullring came to its feet, shouting as the triumphant matador made his tour of the arena.

The young man was already moving. With his thumb he flicked a catch on the band of the amethyst ring. A one-inch needle shot out from the center of the stone.

As he passed the couple, he raised his hands in applause

as everyone else was doing. Directly behind Babbas, he struck the back of the man's neck and kept on moving.

Rev Babbas cursed and slapped the side of his neck. The woman turned. "Rev, what is it?"

"Damn bee, I suppose."

By the time Rev Babbas fell into the *callejon* and Estrella Diego started screaming, the young man was in the parking lot.

SIX

Joey "The Inventor" Bordolo left the flight from Detroit and moved with the crowd through Kansas City International Airport.

At six feet three, wiry and slim, Joey towered above the stolid crowd. With a thatch of unruly blond hair that had just missed being red, and a wide, humorous mouth, he was unmistakably American. Already, in his late twenties, there were faint lines about his mouth and eyes that indicated the ebb and flow of his ready grin. People liked him. He seemed always poised to go out and meet life, to savor and enjoy it. He generated a human warmth. Once he had smiled at them they were unaware that he was not handsome.

Only the very perceptive noticed the unsmiling intensity of his blue eyes or the way his lips could purse into a thin line when he was concentrating.

Joey Bordolo had worked hard all his life to keep his all-American image and play down his Sicilian parentage. The effort had served him well. He was probably the only made button man in America that didn't have an FBI rap sheet under his name.

Only a very few men, mostly high-ranking dons, knew the reason for Joey's nickname, "The Inventor." He had gotten it because of the ingenious variety of tools and methods he had used to kill people.

Bordolo strolled on by the baggage claim area and entered a glass-enclosed telephone booth. He dialed the number from memory.

"Yeah?"

"Joey, from Detroit."

"Take a taxi into town, the Sea of Naples restaurant. Tell the headwaiter your first name, and walk through the kitchen to the rear exit like you own the joint."

"Got it."

"We'll pick you up in the alley."

"Right."

There was a click at the other end of the line.

Bordolo stood outside the telephone booth and lit a cigarette. No one was paying him any undue attention. Casually, he leafed through the Yellow Pages until he found the listing for the Sea of Naples restaurant. Making a mental note of the address, he flipped to the city map in the rear of the book.

He found the street and the correct hundred block, and then found a large intersection six blocks away.

In the taxi he said, "Franklin and Fifth, please. The corner'll be fine."

"Yer first time in Kansas City?"

"Yes, it is."

"What's your line?"

"I'm in extermination."

The cabbie laughed. "Ya mean yer like the Orkin man? Bugs?"

"Something like that, yes," Bordolo said, smiling.

It was early, and except for a couple drinking at the bar, the dimly lit restaurant was deserted. Bordolo murmured his first name only to the headwaiter, who casually indicated the swinging doors into the kitchen and continued to study a reservation list.

After the noise, light, and heat of the kitchen, the alley was a jet-black well of silence. He stood against the wall of the restaurant, his senses straining. His eyes were just beginning to make out dim shapes in the dark, when a hand gripped his upper arm. He was drawn soundlessly toward a battered black sedan. He got into the back seat and the door closed behind him.

His guide had disappeared into the darkness.

The driver, a silhouette against the faint light at the end of the alley, started the car and, with the lights off, coasted rapidly down an incline toward a commercial street. They turned into the street with a roar as the parking lights winked on and the motor accelerated powerfully.

The car took a tortuous route through a confusing maze of streets and braked to a stop before a series of shuttered storefronts. Above the fronts rose ornate five-story apartment façades, semi-elliptical bulwarks extending as far as the eye could see in the dim streetlights.

A figure stepped out from the shadow of a building.

"Come this way."

They entered the dank, close atmosphere of a narrow stairway leading to an upper floor as the sedan pulled away from the curb with a clashing of gears, leaving a blue-gray cloud of exhaust fumes hanging wraithlike in the air.

Bordolo followed the figure up the creaking stairs to a landing. Everywhere in the air he could smell grease and machine oil.

A door was unlocked and pushed open before him. "He's waitin'."

The room was a small machine shop. There were workbenches, metal lathes, vises, and a whole wall of tools hanging in neat, precise order.

A short, chunky man in an expensive dark blue pinstripe hauled his bulk from a battered sofa and crossed the room. He had a scarlet face and a bull neck that strained the collar of his shirt. His thick black hair sprouted from his head like pile on a carpet. Everything about him was big and thick, even his hands. They could have belonged to a bricklayer or a carpenter.

"Joey?"

Bordolo nodded. "The Inventor."

"Sal." They shook hands. "Everything you said you'd need is here. Anything else is below in the garage."

"Our man?"

"They're bringin' him up from Leavenworth by car in the mornin'. Should get here around eleven. They've rented rooms at the Days Inn across from the airport. Here's a floor plan. They got rooms 304, 306, and 308. I attached a pitcher of yer boy to the floor plan. Better burn it."

"I will," Bordolo replied. "You found a place?"

"Yeah. Whore works the airport. Name's Lola, good-lookin' redhead, big tits. I already set ya up with her fer midnight. She thinks it's an all-nighter, five hundred bucks. It's paid. She got a condo at the Airways, sixth floor, C. No problem, good sight lines. Can you get yer shit together by midnight?"

"Shouldn't be a problem. Got my pieces?"

"Over here."

Bordolo followed him to a workbench where everything he had requested had been carefully laid out. He took it all in with one glance.

"Fine. And the uniform?"

"Over here," Sal replied. "We made you a captain, American Airlines. There's one a them regulation bags the pilots carry."

"Looks good," Bordolo said.

"Okay, my man will be downstairs to drive ya to the whore's when yer ready."

Bordolo held out his hand. "Sal."

"Joey. See ya."

The door had barely closed behind the chunky man when Joey stripped to the waist and went to work.

On the workbench was a Lee Enfield .303 rifle, a .38 Colt Cobra pistol, some aluminum tubing, and a box of .303 shells.

He clamped the Enfield into the bench vise and picked up a hacksaw. Taking his time, he cut through the steel barrel and wooden stock just behind the breech. The butt, trigger mechanism, and magazine fell to the floor, where Joey left them. Some grunt would clean up the debris after he was gone.

He cut off the rear sight and filed it smooth. Then he filed the front sight smooth and carefully cleaned and oiled the barrel.

This done, he put the Colt in the vise and sawed off the short barrel. The cylinder came out, leaving the grip with two prongs where the cylinder had rested, the hammer and the trigger mechanism. When the butt was unscrewed, he removed the grips, leaving only the frame. In this he drilled two holes just below the hammer, and paused for a smoke.

He inhaled the whole cigarette in just a few deep drags, field-stripped it, and flushed it down an open commode in the corner of the shop.

From the aluminum stock he fashioned a rod butt with a spring-back T-bar at one end. The other end he split into a fork and drilled holes to match those on the pistol frame. Two flathead bolts held it securely in place. He stopped to survey the product so far.

He now had a shoulder-butt extension to a pistol-firing mechanism that would attach to a high-bore rifle barrel. Broken back down, it would be so many pieces of steel and aluminum junk. In one piece, it could be carried inside his pants leg without a chance of detection.

To each end of the upper prong of the pistol section he riveted a snap clamp. To the rifle barrel, he brazed two clips. When they cooled, he put the whole together.

Eventually an ordinary child's spyglass available in any dime store would be fitted over the rear of the barrel. He had the spyglass, already rigged with cross hairs, in his small carryon bag.

Next, Bordolo opened the box of .303 shells and inspected them with satisfaction. They were lead, unjacketed, illegal for law enforcement and—under the Hague Convention—outlawed for civilized warfare.

Geneva allowed its subscribers to drop flaming jellied gasoline or white phosphorus or bombs on their enemies, but they could not be shot with a lead bullet. The slugs had a tendency to mushroom. Instead of passing through a body, they tended to tear up what they hit.

Joey Bordolo was not technically at war with anybody, and he was far from civilized, so he fired lead bullets without cupro-nickel jackets.

Bordolo dropped three of the slugs into his pocket and

broke the rifle back down, storing the pieces inside his clothes in specially sewn pockets.

With a last look around, he swung the airline pilot's uniform over his shoulder, picked up his flight bag, and went below to find his driver.

The woman who opened the door was a striking redhead with a voluptuous, hourglass figure. She wore a powder-blue quilted silk jacket and a pair of loose blue trousers that could have been pajamas.

"Lola?"

"Well, well, well, they didn't tell me it was gonna be Mr. America. You Joey?"

"I am."

"Come on in, honey."

Bordolo moved past her and walked directly to the window overlooking the street. He counted the windows up and over. Not bad, but a little too much of an angle.

He turned. "Bedroom?"

"Right in there," she said, and giggled. "Wanna drink first?"

"A drink would be fine."

"What's your poison?"

"Sherry."

She roared with laughter. "Sure, I keep some around for my faggot friends."

The bedroom window was just right, the angle perfect. He sighted along his arm and over his finger, and nodded to himself. The target would be in the center room.

He hung the uniform in the closet and opened his bag. From it he took a thin pair of black driving gloves and slipped them on.

"Here you go, champ."

Bordolo took the small glass of sherry and sat on a sofa

facing the bed. Lola, with a beer, lounged on the bed.

"I like that," she said.

"What is that?" he asked, sipping.

"No rush. You paid for all night, you take all night. I like that."

She leaned on her arm. The bed jacket she had been holding around her was unfastened. It fell open, exposing the fullness of a voluptuous bare breast sagging slightly with its own weight. If she was conscious of the exposure, there was absolutely no indication of it in her calm expression.

Bordolo slitted his eyes and smiled.

Lola smiled back and patted the bed beside her. "Why don't you lay down here and get comfy, honey?"

"I'm fine. Do you have an alarm clock?"

"Sure thing." She nodded toward a clock-radio on the bedside stand.

"Would you set it for nine o'clock, please?"

She rolled off the bed and fiddled with the timer on the radio. Then she turned. "Bed now, honey?" She lifted her arms and ran her long fingers like combs through the disheveled mass of red hair. Her coat swung open and Bordolo stared pointedly at the nipples of her breasts. Obviously medically enhanced, they stood out like two missile nose cones.

When he didn't reply, she moved to him and dropped to her knees. "You want to be coaxed a little, is that it, honey?"

Bordolo smiled and set down his empty glass.

Lola unfastened his belt and ran his zipper down. When her hand brought him into the open, he put his own hand on the back of her neck.

"Okay, lover, whatever your little heart desires. You paid for the works."

She didn't resist as he pushed her head down into his lap. His other hand came down in a short, violent chop across the back of her neck.

Lola died silently.

Bordolo pushed her to the floor and undressed. He lay across the bed and was asleep in seconds.

Joey Bordolo awakened when the clock radio clicked, just before the speaker would erupt with raucous music. His hand darted out and shut the machine off.

He lay still for several moments, tensing and relaxing, his eyes focusing on a small dot in the ceiling that could only be seen in his mind.

Fully awake, he rolled from the bed and carefully smoothed out the depression where he had slept. Without a glance at the grotesque, seminude body on the floor, he took the small flight bag into the bathroom.

He removed the gloves and carefully shaved. When his teeth were scrubbed he wiped the room down and pulled the gloves back on.

Back in the bedroom, he assembled the rifle, raised the window, and pulled the drapes until there was an eight-inch gap. When the makeshift sight was attached, he sighted in on all three of the windows across the street, paying particular attention to the center room.

Satisfied, he leaned the rifle against the sill, set out the three bullets in a perfect line, and moved into the kitchen.

He made himself a solid breakfast of eggs, bacon, sliced tomatoes, and toast. He washed it all down with a glass of orange juice and a half-quart of milk. By then the coffee was ready.

Bordolo studiously watched the national news on television as he smoked one cigarette and drank two cups of coffee. He always made it a point to start each day with the

news. He liked to keep up with things. Knowing where
people were in the world often helped with his work.

When the news was over, he cleaned the kitchen, putting everything back in its place.

In the bedroom, he pulled on a pair of lightweight
slacks and a short-sleeved sport shirt. Over that he dressed
in a white dress shirt, a black tie, and the uniform trousers.
The uniform jacket and the bag, open, were set on the bed
in readiness.

He pulled a straight-backed chair up to the window and
slipped a shell into the chamber of the rifle. Traffic on the
street below was heavy, noisy with the departure and arrival of airport traffic.

It was a twenty-minute wait before he saw activity in
the rooms across the street. The door to the center room
opened and two men entered. They checked the room, the
bath, even under the bed, and one of them motioned at the
door.

The target moved into the room, looked around, and
dropped his bag at the foot of the bed. There was no
chance for a mistake. Bordolo had memorized every line of
the man's features.

The three men conferred and then the two agents moved
through the connecting doors to the other rooms. The target
was alone. He removed his jacket, draped it across a chair,
and stretched out on the bed.

Perfect, Joey Bordolo thought, and checked his watch.

Not over one minute.

Exactly sixty minutes later the airport van swung in
from the street and parked in its assigned space. Passengers
flowed from the van into the lobby of the hotel.

Bordolo brought the butt of the rifle up to his shoulder
and peered through the sight. The face of the man on the

bed was slightly blurred, yet clear enough for him to take aim.

When the barrel of the rifle was steady on the sill, he glanced back down to the parking area and the van. Passengers were starting to emerge from the lobby and move toward the van.

His eye returned to the sight. The target's head was centered in the two cross hairs. Bordolo took a deep breath, let it out slowly, and applied a low, steady pressure on the trigger.

He saw the window shatter first, and then the man's head blow apart as though it were a tomato smashed against the wall.

All was a single movement now. Bordolo pocketed the two extra bullets. They were not needed. By the time he reached the bed, the rifle was broken down. The pieces, other than the barrel, were dumped on top of his folded sports jacket. The barrel was shoved down into his belt.

Five seconds later, wearing the uniform jacket, the cap on his head, Joey Bordolo was going out the door. At the end of the hall he dropped the barrel down the garbage chute and listened as it clanked between floors and jammed in one of the bends. It would stay there for days until trash built up behind it.

He went down the stairs to the basement garage and exited by a side door. The rest of the rifle was deposited in a dumpster without pausing a step.

Across the street, the van was nearly loaded.

"Room for one more?" Bordolo called, flashing the driver a wide smile.

"Sure enough."

He sat in the rear seat. By the time he exited the van he had shoved the two extra slugs down into the crack between the back and bottom of the seat.

In a rest room he peeled out of the uniform and put on the sports jacket. The uniform went into the bag and the bag went into the rest room trash container.

As he left the rest room, Bordolo patted the pocket of the sports jacket. In the pocket was a ticket to Hawaii, with a return to Seattle.

Joey's mother lived in Seattle. He would spend a few days with her before booking a flight back to Detroit.

SEVEN

It was dark by the time they made it through the Brenner Pass and hit Sterzing, the first good-sized town in Italy.

"The railroad line crisscrosses the A-13 several times through here," Meyer said. "Want to stop for coffee and a sandwich?"

"How much longer to Fortezza?" Carter asked.

"About sixteen kilometers."

"Let's push on," Carter said, leaning forward and using his glove to clear the windshield where the Opel's defroster had given up.

Outside the car the snow was granular and the tiny crystals of ice reflected the light from the moon. It looked as if someone had scattered a thousand diamonds over the white expanse.

"Think this will get worse?"

Meyer shrugged. "It's winter. We're about ten thousand feet up. It's anybody's guess."

Carter lit a cigarette and dropped back into his own thoughts. Polteri had fallen from the Venice-to-Vienna express. The body had been found by a hunter in the snow about three kilometers outside the mountain village of Fortezza. According to the local prefect of police, the body had been in the snow for about twenty-four hours. It was lucky that it had not been there until spring.

He rolled the window down a few inches to flip the cigarette out. The wind was like ice. The snow was getting worse. Through the windshield it looked like the loneliest road in the world, a winding white ditch edged into the mountains.

The embankments of ice and snow were twice as high as a man's head, and the icy roadway was narrow. Carter was glad they didn't have an American car. The Opel bumped and slid, but it maintained its headway up the steepest grades. At various places, great sidings had been dug out of the banks, presumably so that one car could pull over, and another, coming in the opposite direction, might get by.

"Here we are," Meyer said, slowing the car to a crawl.

And they were. The village had come out of the misty snow like Brigadoon. Meyer followed the directions he had received by phone, and minutes later they pulled up in front of a fine old white stone building. A small brass plaque at the entrance was the only sign.

"Tell you what, my friend," Meyer said, curling his collar up around his ears. "I don't think we'll be going back over that pass tonight."

They entered a large room with a heavily polished red tile floor. A man in a tight-fitting steel-gray uniform rose from a bronze-mounted desk that was probably two hundred years old and bore all the scars.

"I'm Meyer, he's Carter. We're from the embassy in Vienna. Anthony Polteri."

"Yes, sir, the prefect has been expecting you. This

way." They followed him to the second floor and down a narrow hallway. "One moment." They waited. There was a low hum of conversation from behind the door and the man reappeared. "You may go in."

The office was old and ragged but it looked lived in by its owner. There was a scarred wooden desk, a couch, eight or nine gray metal folding chairs with padded seats, two telephones, and a green metal filing cabinet whose drawers were doubly secured by a built-in combination lock and a metal bar that ran through their handles and fastened at the top by a huge padlock.

"Gentlemen, I am Fastoni, District Prefect of Police. Have seats."

Fastoni was big, with a powerful body and severe, uncompromising features. He had a café-au-lait complexion and thin hair that was more straight than wavy. His eyes seemed warm and good-humored even though he greeted them with a sour smile.

"Which of you is Carter?"

"I am," the Killmaster said. "And you may speak Italian if you prefer. Both I and Signor Meyer are fluent."

"Good," Fastoni grunted, and continued to speak as he opened the file cabinet behind him. "I thought I had a suicide or a major accident on my hands, until I found out that the man was a diplomat and attached to your embassy in Vienna. When that happened, I decided to hold off sending everything down to Milan. I was a detective in Rome for twelve years. I learned there that in cases such as this it is better to work together."

Fastoni turned and dropped a plastic bag on the desk between Meyer and Carter. "Signor Polteri's personal effects, those we took off the body. Two suitcases and a briefcase are being held by the railroad authorities in Vienna."

"We appreciate your discretion, signore," Meyer said.

"Have you determined the cause of death?" Carter asked.

"I have it here in medical mumbo-jumbo. In layman's terms, the front of his skull was bashed in. There were many trees in the area where he fell from the train. I suppose we could assume..." Fastoni left it at that with a very Italian shrug.

"You suppose...?" Carter said.

Fastoni sighed. "Gentlemen, may we be blunt with each other?"

"Of course," replied both of them in unison.

"The railroad people in Vienna went through Polteri's luggage. In a false bottom they found twenty thousand American dollars in cash, a Smith and Wesson thirty-eight with a two-inch barrel, and a Beretta nine-millimeter automatic. The Beretta, by the way, was fitted with a silencer. That alone would make me think that Signor Polteri was a very strange diplomat. Don't you agree?"

Meyer and Carter exchanged looks. Carter spoke. "Polteri was CIA."

Fastoni smiled. "I thought as much. Now let me be even more frank, because I want you to handle this and take it off my hands. Here in this small mountain prefect, we are not equipped."

"Equipped for what?" Meyer asked.

"Murder. When you view the body, you will see that exactly half of Signor Polteri's face is freshly shaven. Men do not shave half their faces and then jump off trains. Men do not shave half their faces and dress completely, even put on a topcoat, and go out and accidentally fall off trains."

"No," Carter said dryly, "they don't. Anything else?"

"Yes. The wound was very clean. Our doctor up here is

not an expert, but he thinks it was caused by a single, powerful, straightforward blow."

"By a blunt instrument," Meyer said, "not a tree."

Fastoni reached beneath his jacket and came out with a Walther PI 9mm Parabellum. He flipped it so that he was holding it by the barrel, with the heavy butt facing the two men. "When you see the body, I think you'll agree the blunt instrument could have been something like this."

"Thank you, signore," Carter said.

Fastoni stood. "I'll get the keys to the freezer."

He left, and the two men attacked the plastic bag.

The first was a list of the smaller plastic bags. The victim's pockets had yielded lint and dust of a nondefinitive nature. The cuffless trousers had a little bit more. A couple of seeds that had not been identified, and a film of dust trapped in the vacuum bag.

The shoes, too, had been delicately cleaned and the scrapings of each packaged. The label from inside the coat was from a well-known Viennese tailor.

Meyer whistled. "I knew old Tony lived well, but my, my."

"How's that?" Carter said.

"This tailor's a bit of a crackpot, kind of semiretired, doesn't give a damn if he works or not. Considers every garment he makes a sort of offspring. He charges anywhere from eight hundred to a grand for a suit."

It was Carter's turn to whistle. He went through the rest of the contents. There was a parking ticket from Rome dated noon, two days before. A Rolex watch that brought another whistle from Meyer. A handful of lire change and a money clip containing about three hundred dollars in lire and Austrian schillings. There was also a wallet and a car-rental receipt. Polteri had rented a Porsche in Rome and dropped it off in Venice. Also, a key ring with three keys:

one to a house or apartment, and two car keys.

"Bugger did go first class, didn't he?" Meyer exclaimed.

Carter shrugged. "Not unusual. With as many years as Polteri had in, he probably figured he was due a few perks from the expense account."

The wallet had the usual assortment of credit cards, along with Polteri's cover ID. There were no bills in the money fold. Like so many wallets, this one had a so-called "secret compartment," a flap of leather that lifted out. Carter could feel that there was nothing in the compartment, but when he ran his hand along the flat surface he felt ridges. He curled a nail under the flap and pulled it out.

Worked crudely into the leather with an engraving tool was a number: CS 981 440215 ALC.

"Ring any bells?" Carter said, holding it higher so Meyer could get a good look.

"Oh, yeah. The CS probably stands for Credit Suisse. I'd say it's a bank account number."

Before the two men could discuss the find further, the prefect reentered the room. "The local doctor who acts as our medical examiner, coroner, and just about everything else is still here. He'll give you a look at Polteri's body and then we can sign the papers."

Meyer and Carter followed the Italian into the basement of the building. A young man who looked tired or slightly hungover—or both—awaited them in a room that served as a bare-bones laboratory. Fastoni introduced the man as Dr. Sodi.

The freezer was just that: a good-sized walk-in meat locker that had been converted to a mini-morgue. There were two stainless steel tables side by side with walking room between them. Only one was occupied.

Sodi pulled the coarse sheet down the body.

Carter scanned the wound and then the face. The prominent nose and eyebrows marked a narrow face that was already losing its strong characteristics. The gaping lips, which had never been full, now looked like a razor slash through the gray flesh.

"Well?" Fastoni asked.

Both men nodded. Meyer spoke. "It's Anthony Polteri."

"Doctor," Carter said, "what were the causes of these bruises on the chest and shoulders?"

"Hard to say," came the reply, "but they were made seconds before the blow that killed him. They were pretty severe, as you can see, but there wasn't enough time between the moment they were inflicted and the death blow for the blood to congeal close to the skin."

Carter and Meyer didn't have to exchange words or take note of the look from Fastoni. Tony Polteri had been in some kind of a physical fight just before he was killed.

"I've seen enough," Carter said.

Sodi turned to his boss. "Can I wax him up for shipment?"

"Don't see why not," Fastoni replied, and all of them moved back into the lab room.

Sodi closed the freezer door and turned, one hand digging into the pocket of his green smock. "This should go with his personal effects. It was around his neck." He opened his hand to reveal a rosary.

Meyer took it by two fingers, lifting it until it swung free in the air. "Around his neck?"

The doctor shrugged. "I know."

Fastoni took the rosary. "I'll put it with the rest of his effects."

As they walked back to Fastoni's office, Carter asked Meyer, "What's the big deal with the rosary?"

The other man glanced at him. "You're not Catholic, are you."

"No," Carter replied.

"No Catholic would wear a rosary around his neck. It's akin to sacrilege. A chain with a cross, yes, but no rosary."

In Fastoni's office, they signed the necessary papers and Carter filled in the embassy check for the cost of shipping the body. It would go to Vienna first and then on to America as soon as instructions were received from the next of kin.

"You want the personal effects to go in the box with the body?" Fastoni asked.

"No," Carter replied. "We'll take them."

"There is one more thing," the prefect said. "There was a call a few hours ago from Rome, a woman who claims she was Polteri's fiancée. She requested a claim on the body for burial in case there was no next of kin."

Carter turned to Meyer. "You know anything about a fiancée?"

Meyer shook his head. "But there could have been one. Tony was pretty closemouthed about his personal life."

"You get a name and address?" Carter asked.

Fastoni passed it over: *Isobel Rivoli, Chipardi 12, Roma 5074.*

"I'll check it out," Carter said.

There was no question of going back over the Brenner Pass until morning. The prefect made a phone call and got them into a pension just a few blocks from the police station.

They retrieved their luggage from the car, left it where it was parked, and carried the bags to the pension.

A wave of warm air, rich with the mingled odors of cooking food, beer, and wine engulfed them in the small lobby. They weren't surprised that the owner was German,

dressed in a green Tyrolean suit with carved bone orna-
ments on the lapels.

They checked in and handed their bags over to the son
who carried them up to the rooms. Carter and Meyer entered a small, smoky dining room. A buxom blond waitress
led them to a table set in a bow of leaded windows.

They ordered from a very complete menu, and remained
silent until two huge steins of beer were placed in front of
them.

"You think he uncovered something in Rome?" Meyer
asked.

"Could be," Carter said, nodding. "The secretary at the
embassy said he was in Rome when the word on Rivkin
came in. Maybe that sparked something he was working on
and somebody came out of a hole."

"Out of a hole to kill him," Meyer hissed.

A second round of beer and the wurst and red cabbage
arrived. They ate in silence. Finally Meyer spoke. "What
do you suppose he was doing with a Swiss account?"

"It could be the job," Carter offered.

"Yeah, it could be. Or it could be skimming."

Carter didn't comment on that. "What about the fiancée?"

Meyer shrugged. "I'd be surprised if she was, in reality,
a fiancée. Tony had a lot of women. He enjoyed them, all
of them. Also, he apparently never got over some old love
of his. He got a little glued one night and told me he would
never get married."

Carter cut very carefully into a piece of wurst and
forked it into his mouth. "Talk to me about the rosary."

Meyer laughed. "Wearing a rosary around his neck
would be the kind of thumb-your-nose-at-the-church thing
that Tony would do. He considered all religion in general a
sham, and the Catholic Church in particular a ripoff."

"Then what was he doing with a rosary?"

"Who knows?" Meyer replied. "Maybe making a personal statement to himself by wearing it around his neck."

"That's a little farfetched."

"Herr Carter?" It was the blonde.

"Yes?"

"You have a call from the United States. My father says you can take it in his office."

"Thank you."

She led the way and closed the door behind him.

"Carter here."

"Nick, it's Ginger. Can you hear me? This is a lousy connection."

"We've got a snowstorm here. Go ahead, I can hear you well enough."

"I hope you're sitting down. They got Rivkin in Kansas City."

"What?"

"A professional hit. The shooter got away clean. A rifle from across the street. Blew his head off."

"Jesus," Carter groaned.

"And that's not all. Rev Babbas is dead in Madrid."

Carter's knuckles went white on the phone. "They're moving fast, aren't they? Tony Polteri didn't have an accident. He was killed."

"Any line at all?"

"Nothing definite so far. Listen, I want you to get on the horn to Langley. Check out a Credit Suisse account in Geneva. The number is 981 440215 ALC. See if it's a Company slush account. Also, get in touch with Joe Crifasi on one Isobel Rivoli, address Twelve Chipardi, Rome."

"Will do. Anything else?"

"Yeah. The other two men that Rivkin named . . ."

"Charpek and Evron."

"Right. Have them put under close surveillance. I'll call you as soon as we get back to Vienna." He hung up and lit a cigarette.

Benjamin Rivkin had lit one hell of a fire under someone. Carter wondered, as he headed back toward the dining room, how many more people were going to get burned before he could put it out.

EIGHT

Norman Evron entered Liverpool from the north. In no time he left behind the fashionable residential and commercial areas for the grim streets of the Dockland section. He drove along a row of sooty, decaying buildings and stopped in front of a two-story structure of crumbling brick.

He climbed a dark, narrow flight of stairs to a grimy room over an empty store. The single window was covered by a black shade tacked to the windowframe. The furniture consisted of a canvas cot, a couple of broken chairs, and two stained mattresses on the floor. Plywood partitions more or less closed off a gas range and sink in one corner and a toilet in another. The place smelled of rotted food and human waste.

The man who awaited him in the room wore a short-sleeved shirt and a pair of faded dungarees. Dark hair curled from the neck of the shirt, and both of his powerful arms were covered with tattoos. He was peering through a crack in the black shade and smoking a pipe when Evron entered.

His name was Simon Ellsworth, and he was the skipper of a fishing boat called the *Fat Cat*.

"Thank you for meeting me, Simon."

The man shrugged. "Ya've made me a pretty penny over the years. I've moved a lot of people and goods for ya, and ya always paid well. Where will ya be goin'?"

"Ireland," Evron replied. "I've a place to hole up there for a few months, and then South America."

"Sounds serious. Coppers?"

Evron shook his head. "Worse. How much do you need?"

"For what ya've asked, fifteen hundred quid should do it."

"Done," Evron said, counting the money and handing it over. "When can we sail?"

"Just after dark. This place is a shithole but you'll be safe here."

"It will do fine."

As soon as Ellsworth left, Evron took a shower in the hall bathroom and fell across one of the mattresses on the floor. His dreams were full of the two men who had arrived at his flat in London. They had told him they were from Polteri. Tony needed to see him at once.

Evron knew it was crap. He had not had a face-to-face meeting with Tony Polteri in nine years. It was one of the man's cardinal rules: nothing should ever connect them.

Evron knew everything was over from the way they escorted him down to their car. He was positive when he bolted and they came after him with drawn, silenced automatics. He had gotten away in the narrow streets, but it was only a matter of time. They would hunt until they found him.

But Norman Evron had listened wisely to Tony Polteri: "Always be ready to run. If it ever goes up in smoke, it will go up fast. And there's a good chance it will be both sides after us."

Most of his money was out of the country. He had a half-dozen ways set up constantly to get out himself, and he kept a spare bag with clothes and cash in a locker at Paddington Station at all times. After making a phone call to Ellsworth, Evron had picked up the bag and taken a cab to Stratford. There, he switched plates on two cars and drove one of them to Manchester, where he did it again before driving on to Liverpool.

It was dark when he awoke. He washed and shaved with a razor from his coat pocket. When he was dressed again, he took all the cash from the bag and stuffed it into his pockets.

A slight breeze stirred as he strode down the narrow sidewalk toward a lighted main thoroughfare at the foot of a curving slope. A taxi ride took him across the city to a small tobacco shop. He glanced at the dull metal shutters drawn down and locked over its windows, and rang a bell set in the frame of a door opening onto a staircase landing leading to an upper story.

After several peals of the bell, he heard footsteps descending the staircase. There was a silence followed by the click of a heavy lock. The door opened a few inches, restrained by a length of chain. A short, stocky man with squinting eyes peered out at Evron, breathing asthmatically. "Yes?"

Evron handed him a hundred-pound note with the upper right corner turned down.

"Just a moment." The man unfastened the chain and opened the door. "Up the stairs, please. The room to the left at the top."

Evron walked up the stairs and entered a small, overfurnished room. It was heavy with the stale smell of cooking and tobacco smoke. The man, breathing hard, entered the room behind him and shut the door. He did not invite Evron to sit down. His eyes, revealed in the lamplight, were a watery blue. They appraised Evron shrewdly.

"I believe you called from London."

"Yes."

"You have a passport now?"

"Yes. U.K."

"Good. Please."

Evron handed the passport over. The man inspected it briefly. "Good. What nationality do you wish?"

"Canadian."

"Name?"

"Morris Fuller."

"Occupation?"

"Carpenter."

"Address?"

"One-eleven Queens Drive, Toronto."

"Date and place of birth?"

"Vancouver, April 2, 1940."

"You wish a travel history in it?"

"No. Just bring me into Ireland as of yesterday."

The man took some notes on Evron's appearance. He nodded toward a corner of the room where a camera stood on a tripod between two unlighted floodlamps. "Come over here. I shall take your picture."

When he finished, he immediately went to work. "It shall be about two hours."

"I'll wait."

The man nodded. "There is coffee and brandy there in the kitchen."

Exactly two hours later, the man entered the kitchen and placed a new Canadian passport on the table in front of Evron.

"That will be two thousand pounds." Evron paid and the man moved toward the door. "I shall show you out."

They descended to the street level. The cool, fresh night air swirled about them on the lower landing as the man opened the unchained and unbolted door.

"Good-bye," he said softly.

Evron edged by him and disappeared into a cottonlike mist that had risen from the harbor and was now silently enveloping the city.

They were running in a smooth sea about two miles south of the Isle of Man on a westerly course that would eventually take them into Dundalk Bay on Ireland's east coast.

It was nearly two-thirty in the morning when the trawler passed their bow and slid on into the mist. Fifteen minutes later they heard a powerful engine off somewhere in the darkness.

"What's that?" Evron asked.

"Hard to say," Ellsworth replied, "but it's a lot of power."

"I think it's them," Evron said nervously.

"What?"

"The ones who are after me."

Somewhere ahead a light burst dazzlingly in the darkness. A big searchbeam probed across the water toward the *Fat Cat*. It swung starboard and then came back on the stern. The roar of the engine got louder.

"Can you outrun them?" Evron asked.

"No way. That's a power cruiser."

"That trawler that crossed our bow earlier . . . was it Russian?"

Ellsworth shrugged. "Could have been."

"Then it's them!"

"Shit." Ellsworth went below and came back with what looked like an elephant gun. "Can you handle this?"

"I think so," Evron replied.

"Then get the light. We'll try to lose them in the fog."

Evron went out on deck with the rifle. A faint offshore wind was blowing. The sea was flat and calm. The light grew bigger, brighter. He worked the rifle bolt, drew the butt of the stock against his shoulder, took a breath and held it, and fired. The rifle roared. It had a kick like a drunken mule.

The light splintered, fragmented, and was gone.

The *Fat Cat*'s engine sprang to life. Ellsworth shouted something. They turned fast and Evron almost pitched overboard. Then they were running straight. Evron returned to the cockpit. Ellsworth was pleased with himself. He was chuckling.

"You knew how to use it, all right," he said.

And then a big fat moon peeped out from behind a bank of clouds.

Seconds later there was a chattering, bursting roar behind them. Evron whirled to stare out the open door of the cockpit. Ellsworth began to curse.

They had a machine gun, and they were using it, tracer bullets and all. The tracers made quick leaping arcs low across the water. Too far to port, and then closer, and then on target.

Ellsworth cut the engine a second time. "Christ, we can't mess with that," he grumbled.

They were drifting. The machine gun's busy chattering roar stopped. So did the other boat's engine. Evron could see it in the moonlight as it drifted up. Two men with AK-47 assault rifles were in the bow as it nudged the aft port side of the *Fat Cat*.

"Walk aft with your hands where we can see them!"

Ellsworth obediently put his hands up and left the cockpit. Evron hung back, the rifle at his side. He couldn't see the two men's faces, but he was sure he recognized the voices. They were the same two who had come for him in London.

"You! Move!"

Evron moved aft slowly, but he didn't raise his hands.

"What do you want?" Ellsworth shouted.

One of the rifles went off. Evron dived for the deck as the bullets thudded into Ellsworth's body. He danced wildly backward, crashing against the cockpit bulkhead. He actually made it to his feet once. The tracers found him again. They stitched into his neck and head. Glass shattered behind him. He went down a second time.

The night was suddenly silent, except for the lapping of water against the hull. Since diving for the deck, Evron hadn't moved. The other boat drifted closer. He could hear voices, and they weren't shouting.

"Evron, Norman Evron, stand up where we can see you! This is foolish! We want to take you to safety..."

The Kalashnikov barked again.

Wood splintered all around him. Evron told himself as soon as the machine gun stopped he would get up and dive overboard and stay under as long as he could, swimming, and then surface for air and then go under again and swim again.

But first there was the fear. He could smell it in the stench of cordite, they were that close. He could taste it in his mouth. He could feel it on the deck planking, wet with Ellsworth's blood. He could feel it too whenever wood splinters flew close to his face or against it.

He could stand it no longer. He stood, leaving the rifle on the deck, and raised his hands.

"Don't shoot, don't shoot me!"

"Turn around, keep your hands in the air."

Evron turned. He heard them come aboard.

Then there was another sound, a sharp crack.

But Norman Evron didn't hear that last sound. By that time, the bullet had entered the back of his head, smashing the occipital bone and burying itself deep in his cerebellum. He felt a momentary twinge of pain, and was pitched forward onto the deck. His face smashed down hard breaking the bones of his nose and jaw. Blood flowed out.

The two men, neatly dressed in sport clothes, viewed the fallen body with satisfaction. One turned to the other. "Drag them below. Tie them securely to something solid. We'll scuttle it."

A half hour later, the *Fat Cat* settled on the bottom of the Irish Sea.

NINE

It was midafternoon when they arrived back in Vienna. Carter dropped Meyer at the airport. He would be just in time to grab a flight to Geneva. No matter what the situation was concerning the Swiss account number, Carter wanted all the information on it he could get. Meyer knew a way to bring a little pressure.

From the airport, Carter drove directly to the embassy and searched out Elaine Dermott, the woman who handled all of Polteri's in-house business and served as his liaison with Langley.

Carter hadn't met her before, and he was a little surprised. She was young for the job, a sultry-eyed brunette with a pretty face and an hourglass figure partially covered with a yellow sweater she hadn't washed in Woolite and a short black skirt.

"Here are all the papers. The body is coming in by rail sometime tonight." Carter knew he sounded brusque, but he didn't have time to be anything else. "Did you contact any next of kin?"

She swallowed before she answered and her eyes were getting teary. "He had no one."

"Then get instructions from Langley. You handle it."

"I will."

"What about his place?"

"I had it sealed, as Mr. Meyer requested. The personal belongings were picked up from the railroad station. They are locked in the basement storage room."

"Good, I'll take a look at them. As soon as possible, I want Polteri's records, his travel vouchers, slush expenses, a list of his contacts, everything."

She looked up, startled. The eyes still watered but they didn't look dead anymore. Now they were appraising Carter as if he had just crawled out from under a rock.

"What on earth do you need all that for?"

"Because Tony's dead and he didn't fall off that train."

He heard her gasp, but he was already halfway out the door. He made his way to the ComCenter and put a scramble call through to Washington. Ginger Bateman picked up her private line on the first ring.

"It's me. What have you got?"

"Langley has no record of the Credit Suisse number you gave me. It's not part of their slush."

"Hans Meyer will be at the Du Midi in Geneva. Pass that on to him, will you?"

"Sure. Next item. Crifasi is on the Rivoli woman in Rome. Now, for the bad news. Saul Charpek has disappeared. His secretary said he didn't show up at his office this morning, and his housekeeper hasn't seen him for two days. Ditto for Norman Evron in London. We've got people hunting, but so far nothing."

"Have them stay on it. When you hear from Crifasi, have him pass on to Elaine Dermott here at the embassy."

Carter hung up and headed for the basement. He spent

the next hour going through Polteri's bags. He found nothing of any great interest beyond the fact that the two suits
he found bore the same label as the one the man had been
wearing when he died.

He made tracks back to Elaine Dermott and found her in
a little better shape.

"I'm . . . sorry. Was he really killed?"

"He sure was. Do you know of anything he was working on where someone would want him out of the way?"

"No. We've been really very quiet for quite a while. It
will take me at least a couple of days to get all the material
together that you want."

"Do the best you can. Did Tony have a house here in
Vienna, or an apartment?"

"He just moved into a new apartment about six months
ago. Here's the address."

"We have a man there?"

"Yes, a clerk from the embassy. His name is Tom Lincaid."

Carter headed for the door, then stopped, knowing he
had to ask. "Elaine, how long have you been here?"

"Just over a year. It's my first overseas assignment."

"And how long have you been having an affair with
Tony Polteri?"

She went red, clear to the tips of her ears, but with a
deep breath and a good swallow, she managed to control it.
"It wasn't really an affair, just a now-and-then thing."

"How long?"

"About six months. It started when he moved into the
new apartment. I helped him choose the furniture."

"Do me another favor," Carter said. "Keep your eve-
nings free for the next few days. I might need to pick your
brain, and we might as well do it over dinner."

He opted for a cab instead of the Opel, and gave the

driver Polteri's address. It was five stories, old but completely renovated, in a posh section of the Kartner Ring.

The lobby was a lot of old wood, highly polished, with a big crystal chandelier illuminating it. There was an old-style cage elevator that worked so well Carter guessed it was a new replica of an old model.

There were five flats in the five-story building, all floor-throughs. Carter stepped off on the top floor into a small alcove and rang the bell.

A speaker box by the door squawked. "Who is it?"

"Nick Carter."

Locks clicked, chains dropped, and the door opened. The guy behind it was young and nervous, with dark hornrims and a perfectly tailored Brooks Brothers three-piece in dark pinstripes. He was in his early thirties, but he had aging Foreign Service written all over him.

"Tom Lincaid?"

"Yes, sir, could I see your ID?"

Carter flipped it open, handed it over, and walked across a floor of gleaming inlaid parquet. He went through an air-conditioned living room where the curtains were drawn. The place seemed spotless, the woodwork and tiles polished and shiny. Carter could only glimpse the furniture. It seemed heavy and ornate and somber, even to the crystal chandeliers suspended from the high ceiling.

"Been in Vienna long?" he asked.

"Just over three years," Lincaid said, handing Carter back his credentials case.

"This is a pretty good neighborhood, isn't it?"

Lincaid chuckled. "You can say that again."

"I thought so." Carter nodded toward the phone. "Has that rung since you've been here?"

"Several times. There's an answering machine in the bedroom. I let it take the messages on tape."

"Why don't you go grab some early dinner. I'm going to look around."

"I'd appreciate it. I've been holed up here for nearly twenty-four hours."

Lincaid slipped out the door and Carter wandered into a bar and game room where the wall facing the street was mostly glass with a view clear to the Danube.

There were two bedrooms, guest and master, both as well appointed as the two rooms he'd already passed through. A desk was in the corner of the master bedroom in front of a large window.

Carter started on it.

Polteri's last bank statement showed five thousand and change in schillings. The average balance over six statements was about that figure. There were no letters or correspondence of any kind. In the middle drawer, Carter found a small address book. Most of the names in it were female, now and then a business number in the States or Rome or Vienna: tailors, liquor stores, restaurants, florists, etc.

He noted that there was an Isobel with a Rome number. He was about to pocket it for later referral, when his eye hit on a name different than the others: Susan Safely. Every woman's name in the book was put in with just the first name and a number.

Carter went to the phone. First he ran the tape on the machine back to the beginning and let it play.

— Hang up.

— Hang up.

— Tony, love, it's Daphne. Surprise, surprise, I have a twenty-four-hour layover. I'm at the Inter-Continental. Call, let's play!

— Hang up.

— Tony, Olga. You're a beast. Two divine weekends at

the Szabadsag and then you don't call me for three months. Please, let's get together!

The tape ran silent.

Carter flipped through the address book and found an Olga. He dialed and waited five rings before an accented voice more whiskey than soda breathed into the phone on the other end.

"Hallo?"

"Olga?"

"*Ja*, this is Olga. Who is this?"

Carter killed the connection and frowned at the phone. The voice was the same as Olga on the tape. The Szabadsag was one of the top hotels in Budapest. And Tony had spent two weekends there with this woman.

He flipped over to the page with the Susan Safely number and dialed. He was four digits into the number and there was a click, then a buzz, and the line went back to dial tone.

He tried it again, with the same result, and dialed the operator.

"Operator assistance."

"Yes, I'm having trouble getting a connection. The number I need is one-three-one, one-four, two-six."

"That is not a Vienna number, sir. In fact, there is no one-three-one prefix in Austria. What is your party's name?"

"Safely, Susan Safely."

"One moment."

Carter fumbled a cigarette to his lips and lit it.

"That name is not listed in the Vienna area, sir."

"Thank you."

He hung up and went on the hunt. It took him nearly twenty minutes, but he found the safe beneath an aquarium tank with hidden rollers in the guest room.

The combination—Susan Safely's mythical telephone number—worked.

Inside, he found bricks of nearly new one-hundred-dollar bills. They totaled nearly twenty-five thousand. There was also a bank passbook in the name of Vela Chebsecki. The first deposit date was seven years ago. With subsequent deposits and accrued interest, there was a little over a quarter of a million dollars in the account.

Carter whistled to himself, made a mental note of the address, and slipped it into his pocket with Polteri's address book.

He almost missed the wallet in the back. It was a duplicate of the one Polteri had been carrying on the train. It was empty, but embossed under the bill compartment flap was the same Credit Suisse number.

The last item in the safe was a thin scrapbook. It proved to be a sketchbook of Polteri's life. There were photographs of him in a high school football uniform, at college fraternity parties, in the army in Vietnam, and several shots that appeared to be of a wedding. Polteri stood beside a beautiful dark-haired girl. With them was a sour-faced clergyman.

Carter slipped the spare wallet into his pocket, replaced the book and the money, and relocked the safe. He went through the game room with precision, the living room, and then entered the kitchen.

The swinging doors into the kitchen had scarcely flapped together behind him when an overwhelming smell hit him. He couldn't place it, but it was powerful. Holding his nose, he made a cursory search and headed back to the bar.

He had three fingers of scotch poured and was searching for an ice cube when the phone rang once, clicked, and from the bedroom he could hear Tony Polteri's voice.

"Hello, this is Tony. I'm not in right now to talk to you, but if you will leave your name and number after the tone, I will return your call . . ."

Carter was standing over the phone by the time the tone ended.

"Mr. Carter, this is Elaine Dermott. If you're still there, would you—"

"I'm here, Elaine, what is it?"

"A man called here a few minutes ago asking for you. He wouldn't leave a name."

"But he left a number?" Carter asked.

"Yes, he said he would be there for twenty minutes. If I couldn't get in touch with you in that time, you were to call the same number again at ten o'clock tonight."

"Was his English accented?"

"Yes, very heavy, but I couldn't place it."

"What's the number he gave you?"

She reeled it off and Carter jotted it down. Then he reached into his pocket and retrieved the passbook. "Elaine, does the name Vela Chebsecki mean anything to you?"

"Uh . . . no, I don't think so. No, I'm sure of it. I'd remember a name like that for sure."

"What about One-one-five Brandstrasse, Three-B?" There was a long silence. "Elaine?"

"Yes . . . yes, I know that address. That's Tony's old apartment."

"I see. Listen, Elaine, I know it means extra time, but can you work late on those records? What I really need are the vouchers on travel."

"I'll do the best I can. Where can I reach you if I finish late?"

He gave her the name and number of the pension and told her to use Meyer's name when she asked for him.

"Do you want them tonight if I can get them?"

"It would help."

"I'll do my best."

Carter hung up and dialed the number she had given him. It barely tinkled when it was picked up and he heard Emil Bonlavik's gravelly voice.

"It's me," Carter said.

"I have some names, and by nine tonight I may have another."

"Are you safe?" Carter asked.

"So far, but people still don't want to talk. Can you meet me?"

"Where and when?"

"There is a small café named Sappo's on the road to Schönbrunn. It's frequented by the workers at the palace. Ten o'clock?"

"I'll be there."

Carter hung up, downed his drink, and headed for the kitchen to rinse out the glass. Then he remembered the smell and left the glass on the bar.

Lincaid returned as he headed for the door.

"Hi. Success?"

"Hard to say," Carter replied, slapping the swinging doors into the kitchen. "Who died in there?"

"Oh, yeah," Lincaid said, coughing. "That's my fault. I just moved in when they said I would have to stay here with no relief. So I ate here."

"Yeah?"

"There's a lot of cheese and some Chinese in the garbage disposal. I found out too late that it was on the blink." He shrugged and grinned sheepishly. "I've been trying to clean it out by hand, but my fist is too big. Seems like no matter how much I spray, it still smells . . ."

Carter laughed, patted the younger man on the shoulder,

and moved on through the door. The elevator opened on the lobby floor when it hit him. He held the door in concentration.

New apartment.

New appliances.

Everything in the kitchen and bathrooms hardly used.

Carter hit the button for five, and when the door opened, disregarded the bell and pounded on the door of the flat.

"Yes?"

"Lincaid, it's me again, Carter. Open up."

When the door opened, Carter elbowed past the man and, paying no attention now to the smell, darted into the kitchen. He crouched in front of the sink and yanked the cabinet doors open.

"What's up?"

Carter had the doors open and was sliding under the sink on his back. "Turn the unit on, but not the water."

Lincaid did. There was a steady whirring sound, but Carter couldn't hear the low rumble in the pipes going through the floor into the sewage system.

"Now turn the water on."

Lincaid did, and the only difference in sound that Carter could detect was the gurgling of water in a straight shot through the pipes.

"What are you doing?" Lincaid asked curiously.

"Look around, find me a toolbox or a set of screwdrivers. My guess is they're close by in one of those drawers."

Seconds later, Lincaid knelt beside him unrolling a chamois pouch. "All kinds, little to big."

Carter undid the two clips holding the housing rings and exposed four screws. He went to work with the screwdriver, and moments later started lowering the housing itself.

It was down only a few inches when Carter saw what Polteri had done. A baffle had been soldered onto the mouth of the pipe leading into the chewing knives of the disposal. A bypass pipe had been screwed into the area over the baffle, so that water could drain out but not enter the interior of the disposal itself.

It took only a few more minutes for Carter to get inside the release area of the disposal. There, in an oilskin pouch, he found a safe-deposit box key and a passport for George Nathan Coxe. The Coxe passport had Tony Polteri's photograph on it. Also in the pouch was yet another duplicate leather engraving of the same Swiss bank account number Carter had found in Polteri's wallet.

"Geez, what the hell does this mean?" Lincaid exclaimed.

"For the moment it means nothing," Carter growled.

He got a plastic bag from a drawer and deposited in it everything he had found in Polteri's apartment. Then he handed it to Lincaid.

"I'm leaving," he said. "Ten minutes after I walk out that door, call the embassy. Order a limo and two men. I want both men armed. Take that bag to the embassy and put it in Polteri's office safe. No one sees what's in it. You got that?"

"I got it."

"I hope you do," Carter said, "because if I hear you didn't do it exactly the way I told you to, I'll have your balls in a vise tomorrow. Now lock up behind me."

In the hallway, Carter bypassed the elevator and took the stairs all the way to the basement. By the rear door he found boxes of garbage waiting to be taken out in the morning.

It took only a matter of minutes to rig himself up a small, suitable-looking package from the cartons and let himself into the alley.

Within two blocks of clearing the mouth of the alley, he knew he'd pulled them off Lincaid and had them breathing down his back.

TEN

He entered the tiny reception area and sat down on a stool behind the counter. His eyes were quick and alert as they roamed the darkening street outside the window. A cigarette appeared in his mouth without any apparent motion of his hand or shoulders. He snapped a match on his thumbnail and lit the cigarette.

He heard heavy footsteps on the stairs behind him, but he didn't turn and the expression on his face remained the same. He continued to stare motionless at the street beyond the plate glass window, smoking.

A large woman with gray hair and sad eyes entered from the rear room, carrying a vase filled with flowers. She set the vase down on the counter and leaned over it, her huge breasts spilling across the wood.

"What is it, Stefan? What is troubling you?" She breathed thickly as she spoke.

"Nothing," he murmured, crushing out the cigarette, "it is nothing."

"Would you like a cup of coffee, tea?"

"No, dammit," he hissed, and immediately felt sorry for it. He reached across the counter and patted her arm. "I am sorry, Eula."

"Is it because we haven't heard from Herr Polteri?"

He nodded. "That is part of it." The telephone at his elbow rang and he grabbed it at once. "Pension Prater."

"I'm in, at the Bahnhof. Can we meet?" The female voice was barely a whisper.

"Yes."

"When?"

"Fifteen minutes," he replied, and hung up.

The old woman's eyes were wide and she was smiling. "Herr Polteri?"

"Yes," he lied. "I'm going to the roof. Make sure none of our guests decides to take the air."

"I will, Stefan," she replied, squeezing his arm.

Involuntarily, he cringed.

It is time it ended, he thought. *Eight years has been long enough, too long*. In the last year he had cringed every time she had touched him.

She shuffled behind him up to the locked trapdoor that led out onto the roof. He unlocked it, climbed through, and cringed again at the smile on her aged, wrinkled face as he closed and locked the door from his side.

He walked over seven roofs to the end of the block, and repeated the same process that let him into the top floor of a building of flats. Other than some radio music from one of the flats on the floor below, it was quiet. There were two apartments on the floor. He went to the one marked "A" and rapped twice, paused, and rapped twice again.

The door was opened by a shrunken man with a huge bald head. His face was anemic and thin. He wore stained canvas trousers, a dirty shirt that had once been white, and worn boots.

"Have a beer somewhere. Come back in two hours," the visitor growled.

Without a word the man drew on a shabby coat and left.

Maxim Porchov took a key from his pocket and moved across the studio. The floor was uncarpeted and dirty, littered with an accumulation of cigarette ashes and butts. There were canvases hung on almost every inch of wall space. An easel stood back from the front windows with a half-finished portrait on it.

Porchov opened the door of a storage closet. The inside was large, the hangers hung with expensive suits and casual wear. Twenty pairs of shoes filled a rack on the floor, and sitting beside them were traveling bags of good leather in assorted sizes. In a corner was a small refrigerator.

He opened it and removed two chilled glasses, a bottle of chilled Russian vodka, and red caviar. From a humidor atop a dresser he took a hand-rolled Havana cigar and went back into the studio.

When the cigar was burning to his satisfaction, he poured some vodka and settled back in a rocking chair to wait.

The taxi came to a stop and she paid the driver, tipping him three times the amount necessary.

"You will return in one hour?"

"*Ja, Fräulein.* One hour."

She stepped from the cab and stood as it pulled away. When it was out of sight, she set off walking with a long, almost masculine stride that swung her well-cut skirt to and fro about her equally well-cut legs. Under her right arm she carried, as though in contrast to the smartness of her clothing, a bulging and unsightly dispatch case. It was a vast affair of polished morocco leather, abounding in handles, zip fasteners, and extraneous pockets. It bore a small leather label on which had been neatly tooled in gold the name Anthony Polteri.

She pushed open the door of the corner building and climbed the dingy stairway to the fifth floor. She knocked twice, paused, knocked twice again, and the door opened just long enough for her to slip inside.

Porchov kissed her on both cheeks, took her coat, and motioned to a chair.

"Some vodka?"

"Please. It's freezing outside."

He chuckled. "You have been too long in sunny Italy."

They toasted each other and drank, both of them taking the whole of the glass in one swallow.

"The American agent, Carter, has arrived," Porchov said.

"He went to Fortezza?"

"Yes," Porchov said, nodding, "and probably made arrangements for the body. Our people lost them in the mountains because of a storm. Their car slipped off the road."

"Damn," she hissed.

"No matter. I doubt if Polteri had the list on his person when he left Venice. Carter and a man named Hans Meyer were picked up coming back through the Brenner Pass. Meyer flew to Geneva. Our people are watching Carter here. They have instructions to do what they can."

"And if they don't?"

Porchov spread his arms. "We must rely on you."

"What about Polteri's flat here in Vienna?"

Porchov made a sour face. "They put a young clerk up there before we could get to it."

"They had nearly two days!" she erupted.

"I know, I know, but we had to move cautiously and I didn't have enough people until yesterday."

She narrowed her eyes and looked deeply into his. "You haven't told Moscow about the existence of the list."

He took a deep drag on the cigar and exhaled it slowly. "No, I haven't. I think, my dear, that Tony outfoxed us both. The less Moscow knows, the safer we are at this point."

She grimaced. "As the Americans say, one's ass must be covered at all times."

"Exactly. Don't you agree?"

"Yes, you're right," she said. "If those stupid idiots hadn't killed him . . ."

"A costly mistake, but one we have to live with. There is always the chance that he was bluffing."

"No," she said, pouring again, filling both glasses, "I don't think so. I think I got to know him well enough. He was telling the truth. There is a list."

"Then, my dear, we must find it. What about the brief-case?"

"I've gone over everything in it three times. There is nothing that would lead us directly to where he's put it. I did find this, however."

Porchov took the envelope. Inside was a one-page let-ter, in German. He read it quickly and then checked the front of the envelope. It was blank.

"Dearest Vela," he mused. "It's obviously more than a love letter."

She nodded. "I think he's telling her that the operation is over, that it's time for her to get out. Whoever Vela is, she is probably his contact in Budapest, the person who sets up the refugees to come over."

"Damn the man," Porchov hissed. "He covered himself

at all times. We were lucky, through the years, to get the names of his seven stations on this side."

"Charpek was smooth in Paris."

He nodded. "I know. It was good work. Babbas and Evron were also taken care of as well."

"But we've lost the other four."

"Yes," Porchov grunted, "I am afraid the net is finished."

"Except for that damned list."

"Yes, the list. We'll hold off on this Vela for the time being. If I make a move in Budapest, a report of the request will be sent to Moscow. They will want answers. We'll see what happens in the next twenty-four hours. It may be that our Mr. Carter will do most of it for us."

"What should I do?"

"Go back to Rome. Leave the briefcase with me. I'll go over everything again to make sure you missed nothing."

"What if Carter finds out about you and Eula?"

Porchov shrugged. "He probably will. That old fool, Bonlavik, has been asking questions. We're innocent. If he finds the connections, we'll insist we were just being used."

The woman stood. Porchov helped her into her coat and again kissed her on both cheeks.

"At least," she said, "Moscow cannot say we weren't successful while we were running."

"We were the most successful. But that would be a shambles if the Americans get the list."

She pulled the collar up around her ears and moved to the door. "And if they do, and we can't get it away from them . . ."

Porchov smiled. "I can only say that I am much too old

and you are much too young to spend the rest of our lives in a gulag."

It was even colder when she reached the street, but beneath her clothes she could feel perspiration streaming down her back.

ELEVEN

It was a bad move. Carter had wrongly assumed that there were only the two of them. He could hear their footsteps moving up on him fast now. He was several blocks from Polteri's building. It was time to brace them.

He ducked into an even smaller, darker street and speeded up, looking for a place to make a stand.

That was his bad move. There was a third, probably the German, Otto Franz. Evidently he had gotten in front of Carter and set up his own ambush. Carter was passing a darkened doorway when he sensed rather than saw movement. He tried to roll out of the way, when he was felled by a tremendous crushing blow on the back of his neck.

The blow didn't knock him out. It wasn't the kind of blow that knocks a man out. The knockout strikes some part of the skull, the bony box shielding not too efficiently the body's central switchboard and motor controls. A lesser force landing on the back of the neck, when it doesn't break the spinal cord, stuns the man who takes it. It hurts him, drains his strength, drops him to his knees, leaves

97

him physically weakened but conscious of being hit.

In a daze Carter heard the other two come up fast.

"You didn't kill him?" In German.

"Nein."

"What is that?"

"A box."

"Give it here."

Carter was on his hands and knees, shaking his head to clear away the haze, trying to locate Franz in the misty dark without being too obvious about looking for him. At the edge of his vision he thought he could make out a pair of very large feet.

Behind him, the other two were jabbering in a language Carter recognized but could not understand well, Hebrew. From their tone they must have already ripped the parcel open and found only worthless newspapers.

"What is it?" Franz asked in German.

"Nothing. Search his pockets."

Franz moved forward. Still dully shaking his head, Carter gathered his legs laboriously under him and came up out of the crouch in a rush.

Franz was on the alert. Carter's charge failed to knock him off his feet. But he took a solid butt from Carter's head when he jumped for what he thought would be Carter's exposed back. The blow equalized things between them.

Carter sensed at once that the man had no weapon. His tools were his hands, his feet, his knees, and the hard bone and gristle of his elbows.

For this reason Carter didn't even think of bringing his stiletto into play. He wanted one or all three of them alive. If he could take Franz, he was pretty sure that subduing the other two would be a piece of cake.

After the first rocking smash in the mouth from Carter's head, the Killmaster could not find Franz's face with a telling punch. The man was fast for his squat, powerful body.

Even if the German had given him a chance to use the advantages of greater reach and height, there was not enough light in the dripping darkness to aim a blow at arm's length.

Franz kept boring in to use his squat strength on Carter's body. He was powerful, solid on his feet, unflinching and merciless. Carter, doing his best to return pain for pain and hurt for hurt, fought savagely. Hang on, tie him up, lean on him, ride it out. He crushed Franz's toes beneath his heels. The German, half a head shorter, responded by banging his rocklike skull repeatedly into Carter's face. Neither man said a word, or uttered a sound not wrenched from him by the ferocity of their battle.

But they must have created some noise. The shrill of a blown whistle at the head of the alley where they fought preceded by seconds the approach of a bobbing halo of hazy light through the swirling snow. In the instant, Franz and the other two were gone.

In a piece of light from the flash, Carter saw a uniform.

"Are you all right?" the policeman asked.

Carter spat some blood and nodded. "A lip, my nose, and some bruises. I'll live."

"Did you get a look at them? Did they get anything?"

"Never saw their faces." Carter went through the ritual of patting his pockets. "No, they didn't get anything."

The policeman took a walkie-talkie from his belt. "I'll get you an ambulance, mein Herr."

"No, no, that's all right. Just a cab."

"But, mein Herr, you can't go anywhere looking like that." He flashed his light over Carter's bloody shirt. "And I'll have to have your name."

Carter gave him his ID. "If you'll get me a cab I can make it to the embassy."

The policeman's face changed at once when he saw Carter's credentials. "You are sure you don't want to make a complaint?"

"What good would it do? We couldn't identify them."

"Right. I'll get you a cab."

The man was probably relieved. It didn't look good for diplomats to get beaten up on the streets of his city. If Carter didn't want to make a case out of it, it just made his job that much easier.

From the pain getting out of the cab, Carter knew the German had done a pretty good job on him. The marine guard got very antsy when he checked Carter's ID.

"You want a doctor, sir?"

"No, just point me to the elevator."

Elaine Dermott was much cooler than he would have guessed. She took one look at him, sat him down, and went to work.

Between them they got his sodden coat off, and the bloody shirt beneath it. She brought cold water, warm water, towels, disinfectant, and bandages. While he held cold compresses to the wounds of his face, she sponged his torso clean and wiped him dry. Afterward she bandaged what needed bandaging. The marks on his body wouldn't begin to show for hours, no bones were broken, and he needed no patchwork from the neck down. His face had suffered most of the visible damage: a bad cut over each cheekbone, another at the corner of his mouth, another splitting an eyebrow. One ear was puffed, and several teeth in the front of his mouth were loose.

Franz's most disfiguring blows had been hard elbow smashes to the side of the head, hard butts in the face. It was luck that the smash on the bridge of the nose had been high enough not to break it. Or was it only luck? Too much about the man's attack still required explanation.

When his nose had stopped bleeding and he could breathe easily by not breathing too deeply, he said, "You're not interested in what happened?"

"Of course, but I figure if you want to tell me, you will," she replied calmly.

Carter smiled. It hurt. She was one hell of a lot cooler than he'd thought.

She was putting a bandage over his eyebrow. He could not look up to see her face. "How are you coming with the records?"

"Another couple of hours, give or take, and I should have it all."

She finished with the eyebrow and began on the torn cheek. He still couldn't lift his head to see her expression. When the ear had been cleansed and bandaged, she stood back and surveyed her handiwork. A scowl furrowed her brow.

"That ought to be stitched. I've pulled it together with a piece of tape, but you should see a doctor about it in the morning."

"We'll see," Carter said, and checked his pants. They weren't too bad. The shirt and jacket were beyond repair. "Think you can rustle me up some clothes?"

She nodded and started on the other cheek. "You and Tony are about the same size. He kept some extra clothes here in the office."

Her hands were gentle on his face. She held his head against her bosom, and he could feel her small unconfined breasts rise and fall with her breathing. He resisted a sudden strong urge to put his arms around her body and pull her to him.

"What's the matter?"

"Nothing," he said.

"You jumped. Did I hurt you?"

"No," he chuckled, "you're turning me on."

"Jesus," she groaned, and cleaned up the debris.

A few minutes later she brought him a fresh shirt, a tie, and a jacket. Carter dressed. She had been right. The fit was almost perfect.

"I noticed something when Lincaid came back tonight."

Carter's face froze. "I told him to put that stuff right into the safe."

"He did. It's the inventory from the apartment."

"What about it?"

"Tony had an expensive leather briefcase. It's not here in the office or in the inventory."

"And it's not with the bags in the basement?" Carter asked.

"No."

"Do you think he had it with him in Rome?"

"Yes."

"That means that whoever killed him probably has it. Do you think there was anything in it that was vital?"

She shrugged. "I doubt it. He rarely took anything classified out of the office. Usually the only stuff he carried in the briefcase was personal."

"Like what?"

She shrugged again. "His investments, his deals."

There was something in her tone . . . sarcasm, cynicism. "I hear something in your voice, Elaine. You didn't think too much of Polteri, did you?"

"He was a nice guy and, I think, one hell of a businessman."

"And an agent?"

Her eyes came up and met Carter's. "He was a businessman."

"I see." Carter left it at that and headed for the door.

"Are you going back to the pension?"

"Not directly," he replied. "I've still got to see someone tonight."

As he went down in the elevator, Carter wondered just where Tony Polteri got the money to make all his investments.

TWELVE

They sat in a narrow booth against the far rear wall of the café. Bonlavik ordered a Benedictine. Carter went for coffee.

They both glanced around the room with its carefully preserved aura of Franz Josef. The tourists who packed the place during the day would drink it in with oohs and ahhs. The nighttime customers paid no attention. They saw it every day in their work on the vast grounds of Schönbrunn.

An elderly waiter brought their drinks. When he was gone, Bonlavik turned to Carter. "You ran into a door? Several doors?"

"A buzz saw."

"I don't understand 'buzz saw.'"

"He was shorter than I," Carter said, "but his hands were like teeth."

The old man sighed. "Then it has started. They have a good thing. Nick. They don't want to give it up."

"Explain 'a good thing,'" Carter said, stirring sugar into his coffee.

104

"You have the Jewish Relief and Refugee agency here in Vienna. It is sponsored by Israel and, to a degree, the Western powers. You also have a strong lobby among Western nations that oversees all refugees who want to leave the Iron Curtain countries."

"Yes," Carter said, nodding, "and those are all legal agencies. The ones you helped get out were the ones who couldn't get out legally. They had to be smuggled over and then fed into pipelines across Europe."

Bonlavik took out the list Carter had given him, and smoothed it on the table. "As you can see, I have drawn a line through every individual name and organization on your list."

"And you've added names."

"I'll get to those. All of these people, myself included, got people out because we felt it was our duty. We survived with contributions. Sometimes your intelligence agencies gave us sums of magnitude, when they were interested in someone."

Carter didn't think he liked the way this was going. "Go on."

"That isn't true anymore. Now, if anyone wants out, they pay . . . and they pay a lot."

Carter scanned the names Bonlavik had carefully penned in at the bottom of the list:

— Boris Weiner, magazine publisher, film maker, shop-keeper.

— Eula and Stefan Steforski, innkeepers.

— Olga Sonderchek, hotel and nightclub owner.

"An odd bunch," Carter murmured.

"Isn't it? I know nothing about them. I learned their names from friends I still have on the other side. I do know they all have one thing in common: if they help anyone, they get well paid for it. And right now, Nick, these people have cornered the market."

Carter could tell from the disgusted expression on Bonlavik's face what the old man thought of these people.

"Tell me, Emil, are any of these people connected with the American?"

A shrug. "Perhaps one, perhaps all of them. Or perhaps none of them. Perhaps our mercenary American has his own underground railroad."

The hawklike lines of Carter's deeply tanned face tightened as he tried to put it all together. Olga Sonderchek was probably the *Olga* in Polteri's address book. Carter would start with her, first thing in the morning.

In the meantime, he had a definite feeling of unease, a feeling that Emil Bonlavik was in danger. But before he could say anything, the old man was speaking again.

"There is one more name, Anton Robchek."

"What about him?" Carter asked.

"He was a Czech who emigrated to Budapest. I worked with him for a while years ago. At one time, he was the best. They called him 'the mole.' He could get anyone out. If he couldn't get them out over the frontiers to the West, he would take them out to the East. It was even said that once he took two people from Prague clear across Russia and over the Baltic to Yugoslavia. He was an artist and a genius at forging papers. But even without papers he could still get people out."

"Where is he now?" Carter asked.

"He went to Paris, to study. I heard that he had achieved a small measure of fame for portrait work. But the boulevards of Paris and the cognac sapped his strength and his skill. I thought he was dead."

"But he isn't?"

Bonlavik shook his head. "He came back about three

years ago. The last address anyone had on him from the other side was a residential hotel here in Vienna, the Karlstadt."

"You think he might be forging papers again for one of these?" Carter tapped the inked names at the bottom of the list.

"Let me put it this way. The word from over there is that if these people bring you over and put you into the pipeline, you can disappear without a trace."

"Is this Anton Robchek's work that good?"

"Better."

Carter folded the list and slipped it into his jacket pocket. From another pocket he took a thick roll of bills, divided it in half, and pushed them into Bonlavik's hand under the table.

"You must have a friend somewhere, Emil."

Bonlavik smiled. "There is an old woman in Innsbruck. There is no sex anymore, but she loves the way I scratch her back."

"Go scratch, Emil, until this is all over. If you remember anything else, leave word for me at the embassy."

Carter left the smoky café and walked into the snowy night. There was a cab right in front of the door but he ignored it. He had already been suckered once that night.

Three blocks farther on, he saw a young man and woman getting out of another cab. He crawled into the back as soon as they had paid, and gave the driver the name of his pension.

Nearly into the city on the autobahn, he leaned forward over the seat. "Do you know the Hotel Karlstadt?"

"*Ja.*"

"How far is it from the address I just gave you?"

"Oh, ten, maybe twelve blocks."

"Take me there instead."

His face and body ached like hell and his head hurt, but he wanted to get everything he could out of every waking hour.

The Hotel Karlstadt was near the Danube in one of the oldest surviving sections of Vienna. It wasn't one of the areas where new money had crept in for renovation.

Carter entered the lobby, a long, narrow affair of dim lights and faded brocade chairs. In the dim light he could barely see the dark wood of the reception desk and the clerk behind it.

"We have no vacancies, mein Herr." The clerk was a gaunt young man with steel-rimmed spectacles and sparse, jet-black hair.

"I'm not looking for a room," Carter said. "I'm looking for an old friend by the name of Anton Robchek. He's an artist."

The clerk ran his slender finger down a list of current tenants. "No one here by that name."

"Do you keep any kind of a file on your previous residents?"

"If they were here any length of time, yes. One moment." The young man was old before his time. He shambled, stoop-shouldered, to a wooden file, searched, and came back with a folder. "Herr Robchek came to Vienna from Paris, correct?"

"Yes," Carter said, nodding, "that's right."

"He was with us for a little over a year, off and on. According to this, he was out of town for weeks at a time. And then he was gone, vanished. No forwarding address. We still have some of his things in a storage locker. We are holding it for unpaid rent."

"So you have no idea how I could reach him? There's no mention of a relative or friend?"

"None."

"Thanks," Carter said, dropping a few schillings on the counter, "I'll just have to find him some other way."

Carter was near the door when a voice came out of the darkness. *"Mein Herr."* He turned and saw a very old, very beefy man with a great crest of white hair and pale gray, rheumy eyes. He stood with a slight lean, as though his feet had difficulty supporting him.

"Yes?" Carter said, moving into the shadows toward the man.

"You are an American. What would an American be wanting with Anton Robchek?"

"I'm an old friend. Do you know him?"

"You are not a friend, *mein Herr*. Anton hates Americans. He blames them for not helping Dubcek during the Prague Spring, when the Russian tanks came."

Carter hesitated and then took a stab. "You're right, I don't know the man. But I have reason to believe he is in serious trouble, and I think I can help him."

The man studied Carter intently for a long moment. "Like Anton, I am Czech. I, too, dislike Americans. But I think, over the years, they have done more good than harm. I was with Anton the day before he disappeared. A man had come to see him that morning. I never saw the man, but he put the fear of God in Anton. He also let it slip that the man was Russian. He left later that night and he never came back."

"Do you have any ideas?"

"Do you mean, is Anton dead? I don't know. But if he is alive, and in Vienna, there is one place you may find him."

Something clicked in the back of the Killmaster's mind. "The Café Prague?"

The old man smiled and nodded. "It is the only place in

Vienna that a Czech can get a decent meal. Anton and I used to go there often. When we couldn't pay, the owner would take one of Anton's paintings."

"You've never gone there looking for him?" Carter asked.

The old man shrugged. "Nostalgia gives me heartburn. I never go to the Café Prague anymore."

Carter unwound two large schilling bills from his roll and held them out to the man. The watery gray eyes looked down at them, then up at Carter, and he shook his head.

"Ah, you Americans. It is not always your money we want."

The old man turned and shuffled down the lobby toward the stairs.

It was only a twelve-block walk from the Hotel Karl-stadt to the pension, but halfway there Carter wished he could spot a cab. He was feeling the effects of the earlier encounter, and his body was suddenly wracked with fatigue. He managed to make it, and hauled himself up the stairs.

When he hit the second-floor landing, a door to his right opened and the owner's head popped out. "You have a guest, a woman. She is from your embassy. I let her in."

That was all. The head was gone.

Carter groaned up the rest of the flights and lobbed his hand against the door. "It's me."

It opened and Elaine stepped back with a gasp. "Mr. Carter . . ."

"Think we could make it Nick by now? What's wrong?"

"You lost your tan . . . you're white as a sheet and you're listing to port . . ."

"I'm lucky to be moving at all. A whiskey and a hot bath and I'll be my old self. Whatever that means."

She hesitated, and then moved toward the bathroom. Carter upended a flask from his bag over a glass and swallowed half of it.

He tried to peel out of his jacket and groaned aloud. She was back. "You want some help?"

He grinned. "You've seen me half-naked, you might as well see the rest." He finished the whiskey in the glass.

She flushed slightly. "I grew up with four brothers, and Tony Polteri wasn't the first man I went to bed with."

By the time he had gotten out of his clothes, with her help, the alcohol was beginning to anesthetize the aches and pains.

He carried the flask into the bathroom. The bathwater was hot enough to make coffee with, but after a time he could stand it and slid down until it was up to his neck. He expelled his breath in a long sigh of blessed relief.

"Hey."

"What?"

"Let's talk. Bring a notebook."

She brought her whole briefcase and set it, open, on the floor by the tub. Then she took a pencil and steno pad and, giggling, sat on the commode.

Carter grinned and nodded. "Crazy business, ain't it? You should see when I call a big conference . . . fills a whole hot tub. There's a slip of paper in the inside pocket of my jacket, four names in ink at the bottom. Get me all you can on them first thing in the morning. Concentrate on Olga."

"Are they in Vienna?"

"I think so," he said, and took a hit from the flask.

"Then it should be easy."

"We have anybody reliable working in Budapest?"

She held out her hand and rocked it from side to side. "Lightweights, but they can handle simple stuff."

"See what you can get on a woman named Vela Cheb-secki."

"Any particulars?"

Carter shrugged. "There was a bank passbook in Tony's safe in her name. The balance was close to a quarter mil, American green."

The pencil paused and her eyes came up to meet his. "Tony was shady, wasn't he."

"I think so," Carter admitted. "Question is, how shady . . . and with whose money. Dig into his personal finances. That pad of his cost a bundle. He owned a Porsche, and rented them when he didn't have his own car. His watch was a gold Rolex, and he liked thousand-dollar suits. None of that fits."

"I'll do what I can. You've got a nice body."

It jarred him, but only for a second. "So do you."

They both laughed. "What else?"

"What kind of a lover was Polteri?" The pad slipped from her lap to the floor. "I'm not a voyeur," Carter said, "it's strictly business."

She folded her hands and took a couple of minutes to examine them, the ceiling, and Carter. "He was abstract."

"How so?"

"It was as if he was there physically but not mentally. His equipment worked but his mind was somewhere else. He was proficient but not really interested."

"As if it were all part of the job?"

She thought about this for a second, and then nodded. "That's why it never worked between us. I felt like he was doing me a favor."

"I think I know what you mean. Meyer and Tony were boozing it up one night. Our boy got a little in his cups and confided to Hans that he had an old flame. I found a scrap-book in Tony's safe. There were some wedding pictures in it. Did Tony ever mention that he was married?"

"Not to me. I can check his file."

"Do that, and read between the lines. What about the travel?"

Elaine dived into the briefcase and came out with a computer printout, a very thick computer printout. Carter started at the beginning and went through it page by page.

"How far does this go back?"

"All the way from when he took over the station, twelve years. I had to get special permission to tap into the master at Langley."

"Interesting pattern. The first two years he takes two trips outside his area jurisdiction. Then, suddenly, he's bopping all over the place—Paris, London, Madrid, Brussels, Zurich, Geneva . . . you name it."

Carter scanned it again.

"And there's not a single trip on here to Budapest."

She shrugged. "People in our line of work aren't exactly welcome over there."

"Except I know for a fact that Tony made at least two trips recently to Budapest, and he probably made a lot more."

"I can check Hungarian Intourist. They might give me something."

"Do that," Carter said. "Check under the name George Nathan Coxe, and narrow it down to the Szabadsag Hotel."

"Any suggestions as to cover?"

"Yeah, tell 'em you're Coxe's secretary. Make a reservation for a week's booking, and tell them you want the same room as he had last time. Then, when you've got 'em hooked, get his former charges. Tell 'em it's a tax thing. They'll understand that."

"Why George Nathan Coxe?" Carter told her and her face fell. "My God, what was he involved in?"

"Not enough to pin down yet," Carter said, groaning himself to his feet and reaching for a towel. "But I think it was pretty heavy."

Elaine gathered her briefcase and eyed the flask. "Mind if I pour a drink? I could use it."

"Help yourself."

She grabbed the flask and headed for the other room. Carter dried his body and examined his face in the mirror. The cut above his eyebrow was the worst. He would have to get a stitch or two in the morning.

He returned to the bedroom. Elaine was just finishing her drink. When she heard him, she set the glass down and turned to face him.

"My turn."

"Your turn?" he said quizzically.

"For the shower."

She pulled the gold sweater up over her firm bare breasts and wrestled her arms out of the sleeves. She kicked off the short fur boots, unzipped her jeans, and peeled them down over her lithe thighs and long legs. Carter continued to watch her pensively. From her disinterested, dispassionate expression and her mechanical movements, she was not thinking in terms of a provocative striptease. She was simply a girl taking off her clothes as though there wasn't a man in the room, before going to bed.

When she was down to a pair of lace panties just large enough to cover her pubic hair, she headed for the bathroom.

Carter lay on the bed wondering if she had a toothbrush in her purse. He heard the shower stop and her movements as she dried her body.

Back in the room, she crawled into the bed without a word and reached across him to turn out the light. Then she lay for a time passively, unresponsive. A blast of wind rattled the shutters and a sudden, violent shiver ran through her body.

"Who makes the first move?" she asked.

"You," he replied. "I'm the walking wounded."

Her hand slid down across his belly until she found the lie. "Bullshit."

She rolled to her side and buried her face in his shoulder. Carter could feel the soft pressure of her breasts, and thighs, and her leg gently forcing its way between his.

Polteri was forgotten.

Her lips were opened, sweet, entreating, inviting, and then demanding. Her body trembled as his hand moved to find one velvety firm breast.

She rolled, pushed him back, came over to lie half on top of him. Then she traced erotic paths with her tongue, feverishly deliberate, across his chest, down over his hard-muscled frame, down, down, finally halting to cry out in sounds of pure pleasure.

Her hands curled on his chest, dug into his flesh, scraped along his ribs, and she was consumed with desire, devouring, insatiable.

Finally, cupping his hand over her face, he pulled her to his lips and then moved downward, finding the fullness of her breasts with his mouth, then rolling her back, moving to come onto her soft warmth. She arched her back, rose with him, stretching her neck backward to offer more than mere flesh could offer, give more than mere desire could give.

He stayed with her, brought her close to the trembling brink, listened to her pleading sounds, then pulled her back and stroked the senses again, bringing her closer and closer each time until she was truly in a world within worlds, that ultimate place where she alone could dwell if only for a few, fervid moments.

Suddenly, he felt her hands tighten against him and the scream rose from her throat, whispered at first, then full, echoing from the depths of her to hang in midair, begging, then trailing off to a whimpered protest of passion's temporal intransigence.

She sank down into the bed, clutching him to her until at last she released him to lay beside her, cradling her breast with his hand. She lay unmoving until finally she stirred, turned, her lips pressing into his chest. She stayed that way, as if waiting, gathering new hunger, and then her hands began to move down his body. He started to turn to her and she pressed him back.

"Lie still," she murmured. "Let me have you as I want, my own feast, now."

He lay back and her hands stroked him gently. She moved her body against his, rubbing with feline sensuousness. He lay with eyes half-closed and she did delicious things, soft-flame things, and there was more than simple hunger in her touch as he felt the depths of tenderness and gratitude.

But finally he felt her begin to quiver once more, her body responding to her own ecstasies, the cup of desire overflowing. He turned, pulled her to him, searched out her waiting warmth, and took her once again, this time matching her own gentleness, moving up a path of sweet wildness to the top.

THIRTEEN

Carter heard the alarm and then felt her move to turn it off. Through slitted eyes, he watched her rise, on one elbow first, then swing herself from the bed to stand on long slender legs, long hair trailing down her back.

Regally she stretched and moved toward the bathroom. At the door she paused. "I know you're awake."

"Good for you," he said, letting his eyes pop open.

"Will that old man bring up coffee and croissants?"

"His wife will," Carter said.

"Then call her. We've got a busy day."

She disappeared and Carter reached for the phone. He ordered, and lay there staring at the ceiling and listening to Elaine hum off-key in the shower.

It took only a minute for him to make up his mind. He moved across the room, unlocked the door, and joined her in the shower.

She didn't look surprised. "You've got a black eye."

"Fortunes of war," he said with a grin, and wrapped her in his arms as he moved her against the wall.

117

"Oh, my," she whispered. "Oh, my, my."

Her breasts were soft points pressing into his chest as he raised her legs. They slid around his hips.

"Are you always like this in the morning?" she moaned huskily into his neck.

"Only after being beat up the night before. It adds to my macho image."

Her lips moved lightly along his collarbone, her tongue drawing delicate patterns on his skin. She paused, pressing herself hard against him, opening herself.

He entered her easily. She moaned and lifted a firm breast to his lips. Carter opened his mouth, took it gently, and she gasped and became electric at once. Her muscles tightened in tiny spasms until she was writhing and coiling against him.

"Do you think we'll drown?" she gasped as the water poured over them.

"No chance. We're turning it to steam."

She started to laugh but it turned into a moan of encouragement as he thrust harder.

"Oh, yes, yes, oh, God, yes." He heard her little cries as he moved into the dark warmth of her and her hips thrust toward him. She cried out in a long sigh of ecstasy. He stayed with her as she quivered with successive spasms, each one finding its own climax.

He moved with her, holding her back, slowing her feverish thrustings as impatience and ecstasy fought in her every urgent gasp.

"Oh, God, yes, Nick," she breathed, the urgency holding her voice now. He quickened his body with hers, faster and faster. "Nick!" She pulled the word from her, almost alarm in it, and he stayed his own thrustings for a moment and heard her cry of protest. He came to her again and suddenly she rose, flat belly heaving as the cry tore from her throat to echo in the tiny room, a cry of victory and defeat.

He flowed with her in the moment of timelessness as she quivered, a marvelous prolongation of the senses, until finally she was still, panting against him.

"I hope it takes a long time," she said finally.

"What?"

"To find out what Tony was into. Say, about a year."

Like any good Austrian innkeeper, the Frau had sneaked into the room and left their breakfast without a sound. Over the juice, coffee, and croissants, they outlined the day.

"Is there a doctor on standby at the embassy?"

"There will be if I call."

"Then call," Carter said.

They dressed and hit the street. Carter still didn't feel like fighting Vienna traffic inside the Ring in the Opel, so they cabbed to the embassy.

The doctor, a dapper figure in an excellently tailored dark suit that made him look more like a trial lawyer than a physician, was waiting.

"You look like hell," he said in German.

"I was protecting a lady's honor," Carter quipped.

The doctor chuckled. "I hope you got laid."

He poked and prodded and took some X-rays. While they were being developed, he stitched the slit above Carter's eye. The pictures came back showing no broken bones, and an hour later Carter took the elevator to Polteri's old office.

Elaine looked up as he entered. "Hans Meyer called. He'll be on the four-thirty-two from Geneva."

"Say anything?"

"Dynamite, bloody dynamite. His words. Said he would tell you when he arrived. He'll call from the airport."

"When he calls, tell him I'll meet him at the Café Prague at seven. Anything on the names?"

"Just one so far." She whistled. "Boris Weiner. Boy, is he a winner to take some stock on."

"What do you mean?"

"Your friend's notation...magazine publisher, film maker, shopkeeper?"

"Yeah?" Carter said.

"The magazines are pornography, the worst kind. The films are quadruple-X rated, and the shops he owns are sex supermarkets. My source calls him the Austrian king of pornography."

"Any police record?"

"Lots of indictments, no convictions. It's rumored that a lot of cribs in North Africa are occupied by sweet young things he has supplied. Ugh."

"Takes all kinds," Carter growled. "Got an address and phone?" Elaine handed him a slip of paper with just the tips of two fingers. "Open the safe and get out that plastic bag, will you?"

Carter noted the number on the paper and dialed. The voice that answered was barely a whisper.

"Herr Boris Weiner, bitte."

"Ja, das ist Weiner."

"Herr Weiner, my name is Carter. I represent a distribution company in New York. We have been alerted to the quality of your work, particularly your film work, here in Austria."

"Ja?" Noncommittal.

"We have over five hundred outlets in the States, and we need product very badly...special product, if you know what I mean."

"I see. We would have to discuss this in person."

"Of course," Carter said. "I have an afternoon flight

out. I wonder if I could meet with you right away?"

"I am afraid that would be impossible. I have—"

"Herr Weiner, I am talking in the neighborhood of all your old titles, perhaps a half million or more units a month."

"I do most of my business on this level from my house."

"I understand," Carter said. "Shall we say an hour?"

"That would be fine. The address is—"

"I have it. An hour, Herr Weiner."

Carter hung up. Elaine was staring at him open-mouthed. "What do you know about pornography?"

"That it's boring," he said with a shrug. "But product is product, no matter what it is."

Elaine had the plastic bag open on her desk. Carter dug into it and retrieved the Vela Chebsecki savings passbook, the George Nathan Coxe passport, and the safe-deposit box key.

"You can put it back. I'll call in every hour or so."

"Nick . . ."

"Yeah?"

"Was last night a one-nighter?"

He smiled. "I hope not."

The discreet brass plate beside the thick oaken door read BORIS WEINER. The building was four stories, post-war, and in a top-drawer neighborhood across from Esterhazy Park.

The door lock buzzed, he entered, and as there was nowhere else to go, he climbed the narrow, red-carpeted stairs. At the top, a young black man, in a powder-blue uniform a size too small for his broad shoulders and bulging biceps, blocked the way.

"Your name, mein Herr."

"Carter. I think I have an appointment." He got a welcoming smile full of perfect, pearl-white teeth and a motion to follow.

The man led him along a corridor toward the rear of the building, and opened a door padded with real leather. Carter walked into a large, high-ceilinged room full of soft light, soft furniture, and a subtle blend of perfume, incense, and Turkish tobacco.

For a moment he thought he was alone, but a short, chubby man materialized from an oversize armchair and minced his way across the room.

"Herr Carter, a pleasure to meet you, a great pleasure."

"Herr Weiner." Carter shook the limp, slightly damp hand, and resisted the impulse to wipe his palm on his trousers.

"Sit, sit, please. A drink?"

"Beer, perhaps."

Weiner snapped his fingers. "Nadu, a beer for our guest. My usual."

The black glided toward a bar in the far wall, and Weiner settled into a sofa across from Carter.

Carter wasn't sure what he had expected the king of Austrian pornography to be, but it wasn't this.

Weiner was wearing a fitted, knee-length housecoat that looked as if it had been made out of a Chinese mandarin's coat, and if the heavy gold embroidery was the real thing, he would need a bank vault instead of a closet to keep it in. Under it, he had on black silk slacks and his small feet were encased in black leather pumps. His round face was as smooth as a baby's, and had the same pinkish glow. And it was only the receding hairline that gave away his age.

The drinks were set before them and the black took up a parade rest position by the door.

"Your health, mein Herr."

"Na zdorov'e," Carter responded, and slurped the beer like a longshoreman.

Weiner's big, doelike brown eyes blinked at the Russian but he managed a smile as he sipped something red and syrupy from a long-stemmed glass. When he set it down, he rubbed his pudgy little hands together. "Now, just what is it you're particularly interested in?"

"The young women you buy out of Iron Curtain countries and sell—probably at a huge profit—to North African brothels."

The cupid's-bow lips slitted into a razor-sharp line and the big eyes got very narrow. "Who are you?"

"I told you, Nick Carter."

"I'm afraid, Herr Carter, I'll have to ask you to leave."

"I'm afraid not. Who is your contact, Weiner? Who do you pay?"

The little man snapped his fingers. "Nadu."

The young black moved forward, sure of himself.

Carter stood slowly, his hands up, palms out. "I don't want any trouble."

Nadu relaxed. The heel of Carter's hand caught him flush on the nose. Flesh and bone spread across his features like soft jelly and blood covered the bottom half of his face. He staggered back but didn't go down.

"Kill him, Nadu."

"You shouldn't have said that, little man."

The black hadn't cried out in pain; he hadn't even whimpered. He just smiled through the blood, and a switchblade popped open in his hand with a metallic click.

Nadu feinted quickly, a step forward and a slashing pass with the knife, then a step back. Carter remained motionless, and he chuckled dryly. The laugh stirred the black's anger, and anger made him incautious. He lunged forward, and Carter leaned backward. The man followed, but he didn't keep his feet under himself. He stretched too far with the glinting knife, and allowed himself to become unbalanced. It made him slower, and diminished the span over which he could move the knife.

And the fight was over.

Carter gripped Nadu's right wrist with a quick movement, and kicked. His toe dug into the black's crotch, lifting his feet three inches off the floor. His mouth opened wide and his features twisted in agony. The scream had barely started bubbling from his throat when Carter's left struck, the knuckles twisting and bursting the lips open against the teeth.

Nadu's head snapped back, the scream choking off, and he staggered backward, falling heavily to the floor, clutching his crotch. Carter took two quick steps forward and lifted his right foot. He put his weight on his right heel and twisted it as he brought it down and dug it into the man's guts.

Nadu snapped up to a sitting position, vomit spewing from his mouth. Carter took a step back and kicked him in the face. Vomit and blood spattered as Carter's toe connected, and Nadu slammed back down to a prone position, his head cracking loudly against the floor. Carter took a step forward and stamped his foot down into the man's face. Cartilage and bone crunched under his shoe as he put his weight on it and twisted it. Nadu rolled onto his side, doubled up and jerking convulsively as he vomited, choked, and moaned weakly.

Sweat was rolling down Carter's face and breaking out on his body from the brief, furious exertion, and he was breathing heavily. He wiped his shoe on the man's shirt and looked at Weiner. The man's bottom jaw was headed for his navel, and he looked as if he were about to faint.

Carter's hands itched to squeeze that fat neck, to

squeeze the truth out of him like toothpaste out of a tube.
"Who's your contact, Weiner?"

"I quit, I swear it! I don't do it anymore!" the little man
squeaked.

Carter moved forward quickly and sank his fist into
Weiner's fat stomach. He doubled over, gagging, and
Carter seized his head and brought it down hard while he
brought up his knee. Weiner slumped to the floor, moan-
ing.

"That's not what I asked."

"All right, all right. *Mein Gott*, don't hit me again! I
was getting my girls out of Hamburg and Amsterdam.
About two years ago I got a telephone call from a man . . ."

"His name."

"I don't know, I swear it! He said the government in
Prague and Budapest wanted to get rid of some undesir-
ables, prostitutes. He could set it up. All I had to do was
handle the brokering with my North African clients."

Carter felt sick to his stomach. "What did you pay?"

"Five thousand American for each one. That included
new papers."

"Why did you quit?" Weiner's face flushed and he bit
his lower lip. Carter yanked him forward by his lapels.
"Why?"

"One of the girls, in Tripoli. She was taping pillow talk.
Her customers were army officers. She was some kind of
spy. Two Libyans came and warned me to get out of the
business. To make their point, they bombed one of my
shops. The next time a call came, I turned the man down."

"The man on the phone, did he speak German?"

"Yes, but with a heavy accent."

"What kind of accent?"

"American."

"Did you ever meet him in person?"

"Never," Weiner blubbered. "Everything was done by telephone. The payment was cash, a drop, usually a box at the opera."

Carter turned his face so Weiner couldn't see the look of disgust that had crept into it. "Do you know a woman named Olga Sonderchek?"

"Only by name. She runs a nightclub here in Vienna. That's where Nadu picked up the girls after they came over."

Carter moved to the door. He spoke without looking at the other man. "You're still alive, Weiner. If I ever hear that you're back in the slavery business, I'll be back."

He hit the street and walked until he found a café. Fortified with two shots of whiskey, he called the embassy and was patched right through to Elaine Dermott. She gave him the info on Olga and the Steforski couple.

"Anything from Rome?"

"Not yet," she replied. "I've got the dates on the Szabadsag Hotel in Budapest."

"Shoot."

"George Nathan Coxe stayed there eight times in the last two years. That's as far back as their records go. Six times he was alone. Twice he rented two rooms. I couldn't get the name on the other room."

"Never mind," Carter growled, "I know it. Later."

He hailed a cab with the whiskey boiling in his stomach. Every minute now he was peeling another layer off Tony Polteri's life. And each new layer smelled a little worse than the last.

FOURTEEN

Cabarets in the daytime were like hookers without their makeup and push-up bras: a little drab and saggy.

Der Club Famos was no different, dark and dingy, its hanging vines of plastic flowers looking particularly hollow over chairs and tables pushed into the center of the floor as an elderly man swept around them with an equally elderly broom.

Carter took in the room in one quick glance, saw two arched doorways hung with full-length curtains, one leading to the left, the other the right. An open door in the back revealed a small kitchen. The bar took up the right wall near a small stage. A fat man wearing a blue, open-necked shirt with suspenders hanging down over his trousers sat at a table sorting money. His eyes, looking smaller than they actually were in the folds of his face, fastened themselves on Carter.

"Olga?" Carter said, stepping into the cabaret, moving more quickly now.

"She's not here now. We're closed," the fat man said. "Come back later."

"Business, tell her I'm here. Weiner sent me."

That stopped him for a second. "I'll call Weiner."

"You do that."

The fat man stepped through one of the curtains. Carter went through the other one. There was a narrow, carpeted stairway leading up to a door on the second floor. He started up.

"Hey, what the hell do you think you're doing?"

The fat man started up, Carter came down, feet first. He jammed both heels into the man's face and blood spurted as he staggered back. Carter landed solid on his left foot and drop-kicked his right one right into the fat belly.

It was almost unfair. Carter could see already that the man really had no guts for a fight. He simply stood there, huge fists flailing the air without causing damage. Another crack on the lips broke front teeth and wrung out a panicky call for help as blood cascaded down his chin. It became even easier to evade his wild haymaker blows. Another unanswered cry for assistance gave Carter assurance.

He was bringing one up from the floor that would put the man out for good, when a voice from above stopped him.

"*Mein Gott*, enough! You'll kill the poor bastard. You're good. Want a job?"

Carter let the momentum of his swing spin him around.

He looked up to see a woman at least six feet tall. She had an air of haute couture about her even in the middle of the morning. Golden hair was piled carefully on her head. She wore a conservative green dress that seemed to shimmer over her lissome, full-breasted body.

"You've got to be Olga."

"*Ja*," she said with a nod. "And you?"

"Nick Carter."

"Your German is good but you're not German or Austrian."

"American."

"What do you want?"

"Information," he said.

"You with the police or Interpol?"

"No, but I've got clout."

She moved down the steps closer to him and glanced at the gasping fat man on the floor. "I can see that."

She was on the same step as Carter now and their eyes were on a level. In the good planes of her tanned face there was neither great beauty nor superficial prettiness. Carter saw a dark-eyed directness, enough to charm and make him forget the too-wide mouth and the nose that was perhaps a shade too arched.

"My apartment is next door, in the hotel. We can talk there."

She led him out the curtain and through the one the fat man had gone through initially. Through a door they stepped into a lobby that had an air of faded grandeur and better days. The gilt on the high-scrolled ceiling was peeling, and the carpeting on the winding staircase leading out of the narrow lobby was worn down to the cords. The furniture was massive and lumpy, the upholstery bulged in all the wrong places, and there was an aura of decay in the stained woodwork, the clear-glass light bulbs in the dusty chandeliers, and the gap-toothed railing on the mezzanine above the archaic reception desk.

"This must have been something once," Carter mused.

"I don't own it, I lease," she said, and shrugged.

"There's no entrance to the hotel from the street."

"That's because we only accept customers who spend a little time in the club first."

Then it hit Carter. "A whorehouse?"

She gave him a sharp look. "Don't be so crude. A place of discreet assignations, please. In here."

He followed her into a living room. It was high-ceilinged, with sculptured gilt paneling, French period furniture, and everything but the table and cabinet tops was covered in decorated satin. Olga didn't sit, nor did she ask Carter to. She leaned against a mirrored fireplace mantel, and he went over to a window and gazed down into the street.

"Get it out," she said, "and then be on your way."

"Very well. You made two trips to Budapest with Tony Polteri. Why?"

She laughed. "I don't know any Tony Polteri."

"Bullshit." Carter flipped open his ID and shoved it in her face. "Polteri's dead. While he was alive he ran a smuggling ring bringing people in from the East. What did you have to do with it?"

Color drained from her face and she began to shake visibly. For a moment Carter thought she would topple to the floor. Instead, she managed to stagger to a chair and sit. "Tony's dead?"

"Very. Somebody bashed his head in and tossed him off the Venice-to-Vienna train."

"Mein Gott."

Carter couldn't believe it. She was actually crying. And he was pretty sure they weren't crocodile tears.

"Talk to me, Olga."

She blubbered a little more and then poured it out.

She had worked for Tony in Warsaw years before. She had been a prostitute, and added to her income by passing information. About six years before, she had been caught. Tony Polteri had gotten her to Budapest and from there to Vienna.

In Vienna, he had set her up in this business. The night-club and the hotel both belonged to Tony under another name.

"He was a hell of a good man," she said, finally gathering her emotions under control. "He helped a lot of people."

"Oh?" Carter said.

She nodded. "People who wanted out. He brought out hundreds of people. We used the hotel here as kind of a way station until they could move on."

"A profitable way station."

Olga shrugged. "The money I made out of the place, my half, Tony made me keep. His half went back to helping more people get out."

Carter lit a cigarette and studied her. His gut was telling him that she really believed what she was saying.

"He made a lot of trips to Budapest on his own. Twice he took you with him. Why?"

She looked up at him, her gaze steady. "I wanted to see my daughter."

Carter blinked. "Your daughter?"

She nodded. "She handled everything in the East for us."

"By 'us,'" Carter said, "you mean you and Tony?"

"Yes."

"Who else worked with you over here?"

"No one."

"You don't know Eula and Stefan Steforski?"

"No. I've never heard of them."

"The people you helped. Did you keep a list of names?"

"No," she replied, "I never knew their names."

"Did Tony?"

"I don't know. I don't think so. He said it was better if they just disappeared into a new life."

"Have you ever heard of a man called Anton Robchek?"

"No."

Again he believed her. But it fit. Polteri was playing straight with this one to keep the daughter in line, to keep the other end of the tunnel open and running smoothly. Chances were that the daughter also assumed that she was helping Polteri help her fellow man.

"What's your daughter's name, Olga?"

"Vela. Her name is Vela Chebsecki."

The Pension Prater was a small, old-fashioned hostel on a narrow street near the Ring.

Carter pushed open the door, activating a small bell with a throaty ring, a miniature version of the bells that hung on cows when they're turned loose in the Swiss mountains in summer.

A heavy, gray-haired woman with a pleasant, seamed face and sad eyes came through a curtain behind the desk.

"Guten tag."

"Guten tag. Frau Steforski?"

"Ja."

Carter opened his credentials case and laid it on the tall desk in front of her. "My name is Nick Carter. I'm with the American State Department. I'd like to ask you a few questions."

Her wide eyes grew even wider. "But . . . why me?"

"It's about Tony Polteri."

The face sagged and the eyes grew watery. "I know nothing. I—"

"I think you do, Frau Steforski. Is there somewhere we can speak privately?"

She hesitated for a moment, then nodded. *"Ja,"* she said, resignation in her voice. "In here."

Their private quarters were drab and shabby. Faded

drapes dropped from the window rod, the walls were cracked and discolored, the furniture battered and scuffed, and the carpet worn.

If this woman and her husband were getting rich, Carter thought, they didn't spend it.

"Would you like anything, some coffee?" she offered.

Carter shook his head. "Nothing, thank you. Only information."

The woman sighed and perched nervously on the edge of a chair with her hands in her lap. "So, your government has discovered what we do."

"I'm afraid so," he said, keeping his face a stony mask.

She looked at him pleadingly. "You must not stop it. Tony works so hard, we all do. It is good what we do, to give people their freedom."

Carter slid into a chair near her. "Suppose you tell me the whole story, Frau Steforski," he said gently.

It was fairly simple. It had started about twelve years earlier. She had gotten her brother out, and then his wife and children. Then there were other friends.

One day Polteri had come to her and asked her if she would allow him to use her contacts to get a man named Stefan Steforski out of Hungary. She had agreed.

Stefan had stayed with her for nearly a year. He had worked with Polteri, and they had aided others to escape. Eventually she and Steforski had married. The three of them had streamlined the operation, and since then they had helped hundreds escape from behind the Iron Curtain.

Carter listened intently. "To your knowledge," he asked when she had finished, "was there anyone else involved with Tony over here?"

"No, I don't think so. There was only the woman in Budapest who would hide them until they could be brought over."

"Do you know her name?"

"No. Tony said it was better that we did not know."

A door opened and a short, stocky man with a beard and unruly black hair stepped into the room. He took one long look at Carter and moved to the woman's side. "Eula, what is it?"

She told him in quick, clipped sentences and introduced Carter. Stefan Steforski sighed and slumped on the arm of his wife's chair.

"We have done nothing wrong," he said.

"How much were you paid for each person you brought out?" Carter asked.

They both looked up in alarm. "Paid?" the man said, taken aback. "We were paid nothing, ever. Sometimes Tony would give us small sums. He said they were private donations to help others."

"Did either of you keep a list of the people you helped?"

"No, never," Eula said.

"No, we never did," the husband added.

"Did Tony?"

"I don't think so," she replied. "He often said it was better to let the people simply go their way without a past."

Carter began to feel as if he were hearing a broken record. "Herr Steforski, do you know anything of Polteri keeping a list?"

The man shrugged. "He might have. He never told me. Why?"

"Because," Carter said, "whether you knew it or not, you were smuggling Russian spies over along with the legitimate refugees."

They both erupted at once, soundly denying it. Carter got them calmed down and told them enough to give them some doubts.

"It's impossible," the woman protested. "I'll ask Tony myself. I know he'll deny it."

"He can't," Carter said calmly. "Tony Polteri's dead."

They were both properly shocked. Try as he might, Carter couldn't read anything into their reactions that he didn't think should be there.

He asked about the dead man in Madrid, Rev Babbas, and wanted to know if Tony ever mentioned Saul Charpek or Norman Evron.

Negative.

"How about Isobel Rivoli?"

"Yes," the man said. "He did mention that name. I think he said he was thinking about marrying her."

"He said that?" Carter asked.

Steforski nodded. "Yes. I think they were very close. What will happen now, to us?"

Carter stood. "Nothing that I can see. You've broken no laws. But I might want to ask you a few more questions in the future."

"Of course," they both replied.

The man shook Carter's hand and the woman, tears streaming down her cheeks, walked him to the front door.

"When did it happen . . . with Tony?" Carter told her, and she started, her brow furrowing in confusion. "Oh, no, that couldn't . . ."

"Is something wrong, Frau Steforski?"

She seemed about to say something, then shook her head. "No . . . no, nothing. Good day, Herr Carter."

But there was something wrong. He could sense it, even see it in her eyes and the sudden frown on her face.

"Frau Steforski, if you remember something else, you can reach me at the embassy." He slipped a card into her hand with the embassy number on it.

"Yes, of course. Good day."

The door slammed and through the glass pane Carter could see her plump figure scurrying through the curtain inside.

Herr Herman Neusman, head of the Ringstrasse branch of the Bundesbank, had a bald brown skull and a round brown face that would sag even more as he grew older. He was also an officious, pompous ass. Seated with his age-spotted hands clasped over his temples, he looked like a man on the verge of despair.

"Herr Neusman, you have seen my credentials. I have shown you that I am in possession of the safe-deposit box key and George Nathan Coxe's passport. You have talked with officials of the embassy and they have confirmed that Herr Coxe is deceased and I am handling everything. Herr Neusman, what more do you need?"

The man's head came up, his watery eyes staring at his tormentor through thick, tortoiseshell-framed glasses. "It just isn't done. The order must come through Herr Coxe's heirs and some Austrian authority."

Calmly, Carter stood and moved around the desk. He planted one cheek on the edge of it and leaned his face close to the other man's. He spoke in a low monotone.

"Herr Neusman, I don't have time to go through all that bureaucratic bullshit. Listen closely. Coxe was the cover name for one of our agents. He is dead. Someone bashed his head in. I mean to find out who did it. Whatever is in that box may help me. Understand?"

"I still cannot—"

"Your ass, you can't. Because if you don't, some very bad boys are going to drop around tonight with a pound of plastique explosive and blow your bank to hell to get what I want."

"You wouldn't dare . . ."

"I didn't say me. I won't know anything about it. Now, why don't you march your fat ass into that vault."

The man spit and sputtered a lot, but he marched. When Carter was alone with the box in a small room, he opened the lid.

It contained only one thing: a passport from Uruguay. The name on it was Juan Hernando Morales. The photograph was Tony Polteri.

Carefully folded in the passport was a letter of agreement between Anthony Polteri and the head of the Department of Customs and Immigration in Uruguay, General Eduardo Pelodez. The letter stated that for the sum of one million American dollars, Anthony Polteri could gain citizenship in Uruguay under the name Juan Hernando Morales.

FIFTEEN

The Café Prague was in a workingman's neighborhood of two- and three-story tenements. Violins and concertinas, gypsy music, poured from practically every door and window on the block.

Inside the café a few naked bulbs shed a thin light through a fog of smoke. The low room was filled with sound, disembodied voices talking against each other. From the bar side, a guitar played and a plaintive voice sang about unrequited love.

The men all wore dark beards and rough clothes. The women had scarves on their heads that framed seamed, chalk-white faces. The median age was sixty, and all of them looked as if they didn't really know where they were.

Carter chose a table in the quieter, restaurant side, and ordered slivovitz, a potent plum brandy. He told the huge, bearded waiter that someone was joining him and they would order together.

When his drink came, he cased the room. In this crowd it would be next to impossible to spot Anton Robchek from

Bonlavik's description, but there was always the chance that he might get lucky.

He was halfway through the brandy when he spotted Hans Meyer bursting through the doorway. The man took a few moments for his eyes to adjust to the smoke and gloom before spotting Carter.

There was little doubt from Meyer's excited state that he had struck gold. By the time he slipped into the opposite chair he had already pulled a fist of three-by-five cards from his pocket.

"You look like you just robbed Fort Knox," Carter said, signaling the waiter and spinning his finger between them for a round.

"I just *found* Fort Knox," Meyer announced with a grin, glancing around as the waiter brought their drinks. "Why this place?"

"I'll tell you later. What have you got?"

"The account is fat, somewhere between four and five million dollars. I even got a list of the method of deposits, the payouts, and the string of companies to keep it legal."

Carter smiled. "I thought Swiss accounts were top secret."

"Human frailty," Meyer said, patting his breast pocket. "I got a little black book of it. Even Swiss bank clerks aren't immune."

Carter leaned forward with his elbows on the table. "Five million is a lot to hide."

"It's a Netherlands Antilles company with absentee ownership with a trustee in the Cayman Islands. A Swiss lawyer acted on behalf of the real owner for all the dealings. He acted through a fiduciary account to create another company in Geneva through an anonymous holding at Credit Suisse."

Carter's lips formed a silent whistle. "So the interest

profit on the funds could be constantly rolled over into new investments and make *more* money."

"That's it. All very neat."

"And almost impossible to nail down the real owner of the account."

Grinning from ear to ear, Meyer flipped his cards. "But I found out who it was. You see, there were almost three hundred deposits to the account, but only three payouts."

"I'm listening," Carter said, leaning forward.

"I traced the biggest one to another account. It's set up in some Latin American general's name."

It was Carter's turn to smile. "The amount was an even million, and the general's name was Eduardo Pelodez."

Meyer's mouth dropped. "Yeah. How . . . ?"

"I found this in Polteri's safe-deposit box here in Vienna." He opened the passport and pushed it across the table.

Meyer's eyes took on a cloudy look and his face fell apart. "Jesus Christ, the guy stank all to hell."

Carter went through what he had uncovered about the scam, and added what he could guess. By the time he had finished, Hans Meyer was a wreck. He had shifted from the brandy to straight whiskey and, now, sat with his head in his hands rubbing his temples.

"Oh shit, oh shit, oh shit," he groaned.

"I know. It ain't pretty."

"You know, Nick, I wasn't exactly chummy with Tony. Hell, nobody was. He wasn't that friendly a guy. But I liked him, I really liked him."

"It would seem that just about everybody liked him," Carter said, "and trusted him. That was the secret to a lot of his success."

"Oh shit," Meyer groaned again.

"Elaine Dermott is going over every scrap in the computers and the written files at the embassy. In the last seven years or so, Polteri turned over a ton of information and several people. About two percent of it, at the most, was worth a damn."

"The Russians were working with him?"

"It sure as hell looks that way. But from the amount of money, it looks to me like he was an independent contractor. He set the deal up and used people."

"Even this Weiner character," Meyer growled. "Jesus, white slavery."

"Evidently, Tony had two sides, dark and darkest. He saw a way to pick up change from Weiner, and took it."

"What about this Olga Sonderchek and the Steforski couple? Can you believe them?"

Carter shrugged. "So far I have no reason not to. On the surface it appears that Polteri was playing them all like a harp. They honestly didn't know what he was really up to."

Meyer sighed. "Well, I guess you never know. What next?"

"For you, Budapest. I want you to take this Olga Sonderchek with you."

"The daughter, what's her name?"

"Vela Chebsecki. Bleed her, Hans. Get everything you can, and don't leave until you're sure you've got it all and she's telling you the truth."

Meyer snapped his fingers. "Other than Polteri, she was the only one who handled everyone he brought over."

"Right. She just might have made a list of names, descriptions. Something."

"Then you think there is a list?"

"I don't know," Carter replied with a sigh. "But I'll tell you this. Tony Polteri had this engineered down to the last detail, his escape. He might have worked with the Russians, but I doubt if he trusted them."

"Insurance?" Meyer said.

"You got it."

"Then why would they kill him?"

"Good question," Carter said, "and right, except for the existence of a list, that's the big mystery."

"I'll leave first thing in the morning for Budapest. You?"

"So far we seem to have nailed everybody down except this friend in Rome. Joe Crifasi called Elaine. He's got her pegged. I fly to Rome tomorrow afternoon."

They had ordered *husa* with sauerkraut and dumplings. It was hardly touched when they stood to leave. During the conversation both of them had lost their appetites.

"Where are you headed now?" Carter asked when they hit the street.

"Back to the embassy, cab."

"Drop me off on the way. And, Hans, starting tomorrow night, have a man on this place every night through the dinner hour."

"Robchek?"

"Yeah. I doubt we'll have any luck, but he could be a coup if we got our hands on him."

In the cab, halfway between the Café Prague and the embassy, Meyer let out another low groan.

"What is it?" Carter asked.

"Just remembered what you said about Polteri having two sides, dark and darkest."

"Yeah?"

"He must have had a little bit of a third, lighter side."

"Why?"

"Because the other two payouts on that Swiss account?

They were good-sized, both nearly half a million each, to some Catholic kids' charity in Rome."

"Maybe that goes along with the rosary we found."

"Like he hated his own guts so much for what he was doing that he suddenly found religion?"

Carter shrugged. "It takes all kinds."

A bar of light from the cracked door fell across the space between the twin beds. In one of them, Stefan Steforski breathed easily. In the other, his wife rolled from side to side in sleeplessness.

Finally she sat up and swung her feet to the floor. "Stefan . . . Stefan?"

"Yes, yes, what is it?" he groaned irritably when she'd roused him.

"Do you think we have actually smuggled Russian spies into the West?"

"For God's sake, Eula, go to sleep."

"Do you?"

"Of course not. Herr Polteri was a U.S. government agent. Why would he smuggle enemies of his country into the West?"

"I don't know." She sat pensively for several moments, picking absently at the long, heavy nightgown that covered her legs clear to the ankles. "Stefan . . . ?"

"What is it now?"

"Do you have another woman, a mistress?"

He rolled over, anger suffusing his face. Suddenly it turned to laughter. "A mistress? At my age? Woman, are you out of your mind?"

"I realize that there has never been a great deal between us. We were just an old man and an old woman thrown together . . ."

"Eula, be sensible."

"You have an apartment in the corner building, don't you? I saw you come out of there once, all dressed. It was when you were going on one of your trips."

Now he was sweating, his mind racing. "Yes, Eula, I do have an apartment there. That is where I meet our contacts."

"Like Herr Polteri?"

"Yes."

"I thought you met them on the roof."

"Sometimes," he hissed. "Sometimes I meet them on the roof. Sometimes in the apartment."

"Where do you go on all your trips, Stefan?"

"For God's sake, woman, you know where I go! I do errands for Herr Polteri. Now go to sleep. It's Fräulein Posener's late day tomorrow. I have to get up early."

Eula lay back on her bed. She was about to ask him another question, but she could sense the violent anger in his voice.

She asked the question in her mind: *Stefan, why did you lie to me the other night? You didn't go on the roof or to the apartment to meet Tony Polteri. According to Herr Carter, Herr Polteri had already been dead for three days. And on the night he was killed, Stefan, you were on one of your trips.*

She lay quiet for nearly an hour, until she was sure the breathing was deep and normal from the other bed. Then she soundlessly slipped from the bed and moved across the room and out the door.

She found the card on the desk in the office. In the moonlight coming through the small window, she read the number and dialed.

A bored night duty officer's voice answered. "American embassy, Sergeant Parker speaking."

"*Ja*, my name is Eula Steforski. I want to leave a message for—"

The phone was yanked from her hand and slammed back down onto its cradle. She tried to turn, but a heavy arm came around her neck.

Suddenly she was gasping for air. A knee was jammed painfully into her lower back. She tried to scream but no sound would come.

And then she couldn't breathe at all.

Her last thoughts just before her spine at the base of her neck cracked were: *Why, Stefan? Why do you help them all these years? Who are you, Stefan?*

Breathing heavily, General Maxim Porchov dragged the heavy body into the hall and paused. There was only one room occupied for the night, a woman and her young son. They were on the very top floor. There was little chance that they had heard a thing.

He opened the door to the cellar and, grunting with the effort, managed to struggle the old woman down the stairs.

It took him nearly an hour to pry the floorboards up in the storeroom and dig a shallow grave. A half hour after that, the grave was covered and the floorboards replaced, with old food cartons over the spot.

Back in the office, he dialed the phone and a sleepy female voice answered on the fifth ring.

"*Ja?*"

"Fräulein Posener, I am sorry to awaken you at such an hour."

"Herr Steforski?"

"We have a little emergency here."

"What has happened?"

"A good friend of ours in Salzburg, he has had a heart attack."

"Oh, no . . ."

"*Ja, ja*, a terrible thing. Eula and I must go at once, tonight. I wonder if you would mind coming in early tomorrow?"

"No, no, of course I wouldn't mind. How long will you be?"

"I imagine at least a week. Perhaps you should move in, take one of the rooms for that time."

"Don't worry, *mein Herr*, I will take care of everything."

"*Danke, Fräulein, danke.*"

He hung up and dashed back to their quarters. He carefully packed himself a bag and another for his dead wife. Then he made his way to the roof.

Carter had rolled and tossed for nearly an hour before he had finally fallen asleep. The sound of the door opening gently awakened him. He didn't move anything but one eyelid.

He smelled the perfume even before she stepped into the pool of moonlight sifting through the curtains. "How did you get in here?"

"You gave me a set of keys this morning, don't you remember?"

"I do now," he said groggily.

She began to undress, talking all the while. "I saw Hans before I left the embassy."

"Yeah?"

"He told me everything." She kicked her shoes off and pulled her dress up over her head. "God, Tony was a bastard."

"He was that."

The dress landed in a chair and she turned to him in overflowing bra and white nylon panties. "I'm almost through his personal stuff, bank account here in Vienna, letters . . ."

"Anything?" Carter asked, feeling sleep start to claim him again.

"A few charities in the States, lots of flowers on a regular basis. I suppose they're for old girl friends." Her hair loosened to her shoulders and her breasts burst free as the bra came away. "By the way, Tony was married once."

"Oh?"

"Yeah, it was annulled. I've got the FBI doing some checking." She slid the panties down to her ankles, kicked them off, and crawled into the bed, cuddling her naked body to his.

"Hey, wanna fool around?"

Carter was sound asleep.

SIXTEEN

The day was crisp and bright. Sunlight in Rome is golden, and now it glinted off the mustard-colored walls of the old buildings they passed from the airport into the city.

Another fifteen minutes of swirling through growling motorcycles and honking cars, and the taxi was on the Via del Corso. Two blocks farther and Carter leaned forward. "This is fine."

He paid the driver and, clutching his small overnight bag, trudged up the slight incline to the café. With a sigh he dropped into one of the chairs at an outside table. A white-jacketed waiter instantly appeared.

"Campari."

"*Sì, signore*, at once." The waiter returned with the drink and placed it before Carter with a small paper napkin. Carter took a guidebook from his pocket and pretended to study it as he sipped his drink.

It was four-thirty.

At five o'clock, Joe Crifasi, AXE liaison in Rome, dropped into the chair beside him.

"You're late," Carter said without looking up. "I'll never get any sightseeing done at this rate."

Crifasi yawned. "The fucking traffic is worse than Los Angeles. What's that?"

"Campari."

"Ugh. Bring me one of those," he said to the waiter who had appeared at his side. "What's the scoop on Tony Polteri?"

"He's dead."

"I know that, for crissakes."

"He was also dirty."

"Oh no."

"Oh yes." Carter told him everything he had been able to learn up to that point.

"My God," Crifasi growled. "And Polteri was behind it all?"

"Looks that way," Carter said. "How often did you see him when he was in Rome?"

Crifasi shrugged. "Never."

"'Nuf said," Carter replied. "Evidently this Isobel Rivoli was his connection down here. What have you got on her?"

"I'm glad you're sitting down," Crifasi said.

"Why?"

"Because she's a Mossad agent."

Crifasi had a dark green Lancia sedan. They drove out of the crowded city, across a narrow bridge spanning the Tiber, and onto the highway lined with pine trees leading to Ostia and the Tyrrhenian Sea. The farther they went, the posher the area.

Carter commented. "This Isobel Rivoli must make a buck or two."

Crifasi never took his eyes off the road. "She's more than just a singer in the Café Med."

"How much more?"

"She *owns* the Café Med. It's all there, in the file."

The Killmaster opened the manila folder. The file was thin, two typed pages, no picture.

Isobel Rivoli was orginally Isobel Gedalia. She was the daughter of Zeb and Hannah Gedalia, born in Minsk. The father was a professor of languages at the University in Minsk, and a closet Zionist. The entire family had been arrested when Isobel was about twelve, and shipped off to a Siberian village.

They became nonpersons for three years, and then a fairly powerful Jewish merchant banker in Rome had started a major lobbying campaign to have them released. Eventually the mother and daughter were released through the Jewish refugee program in Vienna. They moved on to Tel Aviv. A year later, the mother, Hannah, was killed in an automobile accident.

Isobel Gedalia, now seventeen, had exhibited considerable musical talent. She applied for an apprentice position at the Milan opera, and got it.

"Who was the merchant banker in Rome who helped get them out?" Carter asked.

"His name is Morris Epstein," Crifasi replied. "He probably had something to do with Isobel getting into La Scala."

"Where is he now?"

"He died about two years ago."

"Anything in depth on him?" Carter asked.

"Very little. He was rich, made most of his money in brokering oil. He had a lot of connections with rich Greeks, shipping. He also had a lengthy record of donating to Zionist causes. He lived simply for a rich man, no family. When he died, most of his money went to Jewish refugee and relief funds."

"Any reason to believe he wasn't straight?"

"None that I could find," Crifasi replied. "There's the Café Med."

Carter noted the area and the address as they passed, and scanned the last sheet of the file.

Isobel never made it in opera. She started working as a pop singer in Rome and acquired somewhat of a following.

Five years earlier she had married Enrico Rivoli, a man thirty-five years her senior. He had lasted eighteen months. All his holdings—including the Café Med—had gone to Isobel.

"There's damn little in here about her and Mossad," Carter murmured.

Crifasi shrugged. "That's because I found out damn little. I called in an old IOU from their station head in Athens, but he was tight-lipped."

"But she is for real?"

"According to him. Where and how she was recruited, I don't know. What she's done for them in the past, I don't know. What she's into now, I don't know."

"But you're sure she's legit?" Carter pressed.

"She's legit. Not on the payroll, but she wouldn't need the money. There's her building."

It was eight stories with a lot of marble in front and a doorman in gaudy livery. It adjoined a taller building on the left and an alley on the right.

"She owns the whole building," Crifasi said, "and lives in the penthouse, eighth floor."

Carter whistled. If she was working with Polteri, he thought, she could probably afford all this. "How much did her husband leave her?"

"Lots," Crifasi replied. "More than she could ever spend."

"So much for that theory."

"What theory?"

"Never mind. I've seen enough."

Crifasi made a U-turn and headed back toward the center of the city. Still on the outskirts, he cut off onto a small road that climbed into the hills. Minutes later he turned into a cobbled drive between a pair of marble gates.

"What's this?" Carter asked.

"Your abode. The owner's a friend, on business in New York. I didn't think you'd want to use the regular places or a hotel."

"Good thinking."

The villa was a small, exquisite, miniature duplicate of a Roman palazzo. During the years, the red brick had weathered to a soft ochre and the fluted marble columns of the portico extending along the front were a luminous pearl-gray.

"Nice," Carter said dryly, dropping his bag in the enormous master bedroom.

"For safety's sake, the servants are on holiday while you're here. The bar is stocked, and I'll leave the Lancia for you. There's a Fiat in the garage I can use."

"Does the phone work?"

Crifasi nodded. "Yeah, and it was checked this morning. I've got a lot going down in the next couple of days, but if you get in a bind, call me."

"Shouldn't be necessary," Carter said. "Joe . . ."

"Yeah?"

"The owner . . . male or female?"

Crifasi grinned. "Need you ask?"

He left and Carter called Vienna. Elaine Dermott was gone for the day. There were no messages for him from

Meyer. He called Elaine's apartment and there was no answer.

He unpacked, showered, and shaved. Then, with a drink, he moved to the front windows and checked the area.

Nothing.

He hadn't spotted them in Vienna, but his sixth sense had told him that every move he made had been noted.

That same sense had told him that they had dropped him at the airport and not bothered to pick him up again in Rome.

Why?

He paged through a telephone book and dialed.

"Café Med."

"I'd like to make a reservation for dinner tonight. One."

"Sì, signore. The time?"

"What time are the shows?"

"At ten and midnight."

"Ten will be fine," Carter said, and gave his name.

He hung up and stretched across the vast bed, his mind clicking through what he had learned.

Isobel Rivoli fit the pattern of Polteri's imports. But she had come over before Polteri was really set up in business.

Also, the Mossad made damn few mistakes. If she was an agent, they would have checked everything down to the last detail.

Still, every agency in the world makes a mistake now and then.

Look at Tony Polteri.

SEVENTEEN

The Café Med was big and top-drawer. The marquee announced a complete "Parisian floor show," and featured Isobel Rivoli. Inside, the lights were dim, the furnishings in a motif of the sea, and, from the cover, the prices stiff. Wide lengths of fishnet hung from open beams with starfish attached. The mâitre d' was in a tux.

"Good evening, signore. You have a reservation?"

"Carter, one."

He turned Carter over to a petite hostess bulging out of an abbreviated sailor suit. "This way. Please watch your step. It's dim until you get used to the lighting."

Carter followed the hostess's surefooted stride to a private booth with more fishnet. Two waiters materialized at once. He ordered a Chivas to start, seafood ravioli, a veal dish, and a bottle of good red.

His entree arrived just as the show started. The dinner was excellent, the show even better, with top-grade performers and new acts. The nudes were very nude and very lovely.

Just as coffee and brandy arrived, a pinspot came up on the stage and Isobel Rivoli stepped into it.

She was good right from the first lyric out of her mouth. The song was lilting Italian, about a girl who fed the pigeons on the Spanish Steps, grew up, found true love, lost it, and fed some more pigeons.

Isobel Rivoli actually made you believe it.

Her beauty helped. She had deep black liquid eyes that looked at each man as though she were his and only his. Her very long hair, which had been brushed until it gleamed like satin, was parted in the center and hung loosely down her back almost to her knees. Her skin was silken smooth. The sheer white peasant blouse was cut deeply, revealing the top of her perfectly rounded breasts, which rose enticingly as she sang. Her waist was slim, encircled by a wide leather belt above a black skirt that revealed her slightly full hips. The slit on the right side exposed her exquisitely shaped legs. The movement of her body became feline.

When she finished, the applause was tumultuous. She tossed her mane of ebony hair and laughed, parting the extraordinary red sculptured lips.

Applause brought her back for an encore. It was a medley in French, Spanish, and English. By the time she finished, Carter was sure that one aspect of Isobel Rivoli's cover was not phony: her talent.

He paid and headed for the parking lot. The show was close to an hour long, with her segment nearly half. He guessed that she wouldn't leave the club much before two in the morning.

More than enough time.

He circled the block twice. In the lobby, the night doorman lounged with a newspaper. The street was quiet.

He parked three blocks away and strolled back casually,

finally slipping into the inky blackness of a doorway he
had spotted earlier from the car.

As far as Carter could see there were no lights on in the
penthouse. Isobel Rivoli didn't have houseguests.

He returned to the car and pulled off his coat and jacket
as he climbed into the back. Off came his shoes, to be
replaced by black sneakers. A black turtleneck over his
black slacks completed the outfit. A short steel jimmy and
pair of wire cutters went into his back pocket, and he slid
the Luger into his belt under the turtleneck.

He walked quickly around the block and approached the
apartment building from the rear. The lock on the back
door required several tense minutes to jimmy. He closed
the door, and as the lock was opened inside with a knob, he
locked it. He ran silently along the passage to the entrance
to the stairs and climbed the eight flights at a slow, steady
pace to conserve his wind.

At the top landing, a narrow concrete stairway led to the
roof. It required another lengthy period of time to unlock
the iron door at the top, and he wondered if he was losing
his touch.

He climbed out onto the roof and breathed deeply of the
cool night air, and surveyed the lights of the Eternal City
spread out like a carpet of jewels.

There was a waist-high parapet buit along the edge of
the center section of the roof, and eight feet below it, the
terrace. Carter leaned down and searched the top fronds of
the potted palms screening the wall, and smiled grimly.
Five strands of barbed wire were fastened to iron bars
sticking straight out from the wall a couple of feet below
him. He snipped the wires close to a bar and bent the loose
ends back. He dropped lightly onto the tiles of the terrace.

The floor-to-ceiling picture windows along the front
were closed, but as the drapes were not drawn, he could

make out the vague outline of living room furniture in the darkness. Carefully, avoiding the collection of iron chairs and tables and the containers for the collection of plants scattered about the terrace, he made his way around to the side.

There was a pair of French doors and beyond them, a row of ordinary windows. There wasn't a glimmer of light from any of them.

The French doors were bolted inside, and after a quick inspection with the flashlight, Carter left them. The fastenings were solid, and in the complete silence the noise he would make opening them with the jimmy would surely be heard.

He checked each window along the side and the last one was open a few inches. He pulled it out farther, climbed over the sill onto a kitchen table, and dropped to the floor like a cat. Isobel, he was thinking, was careless. Or else there was nothing in her apartment worth stealing.

He had to use the flashlight momentarily in the short corridor that led into the large vestibule. To the left was the main entrance to the apartment, and beyond, an open arch into the living room.

Moving quickly, he lifted a corner of each of the three modern paintings and saw nothing that resembled a wall safe. The drawer in the desk contained writing paper and a collection of ballpoints. The ornate Florentine leather letter folder on the top was empty, and the two antique silver boxes contained nothing of interest. He straightened up and looked around.

What was it?

And then it hit him. There was nothing *personal* in the room . . . no photographs, no letters in the desk, not even an address book. It was a transient room used for stopovers rather than permanent living. Even the furnishings were decorative rather than utilitarian.

He moved on to the bedroom. He started with the top drawers of the dresser. They revealed little other than the fact that Isobel Rivoli liked expensive, sexy lingerie and lots of sweaters. The closet was a hodgepodge of designer gowns and dresses and well-worn jeans. As in any woman's closet, the floor was lined with shoes. But the only pair that looked used was a pair of Reebok running shoes.

Proving nothing, Carter thought, except that she liked to relax at home.

He hit the second bedroom next, and again came up empty; the den the same, almost. In a shallow drawer behind the bar beneath some towels, he found a chrome-plated .38 revolver. Not exactly a lady's gun, unless the lady knew what she was doing.

He removed the shells, dropped them into his pocket, and replaced the gun.

The last room was the kitchen. Standing in the center, leaning against a huge butcher-block table, he remembered and smiled.

The water sounded the same through the taps, with or without the disposal being turned on. A knife served as a screwdriver, and in minutes he had the main housing of the garbage disposal dropped and open.

"Well, well," he said aloud. "I wonder who took lessons from whom."

Inside, in watertight packages, he found twenty thousand American dollars in tight rolls, and four passports. The passports were in four different names and nationalities: French, German, American, and Austrian. Isobel Rivoli's photograph was on all of them.

But the most interesting thing about them was the fact that they were all authentic.

Carter got out his notebook and pen. He copied down all the entry and exit stamps from each of them and then put everything back.

When he was done, he went back into the den and fixed himself a drink. Then, taking the bottle with him, he went into the living room and sat down to wait.

Hans Meyer sat on a bench in Lido Park, nervously smoking, his eyes scanning the people moving down the broad walks. Then he saw her, standing in the shadows about twenty yards away, staring openly at him.

Her eyes darted to the people on the other benches and then grew wide as two uniformed policemen passed. Suddenly she moved farther into the shadows.

Meyer looked away, as if his gaze would frighten her. The two uniforms exited the park, and out of the corner of his eye Meyer saw her begin a casual stroll in his direction. During her leisurely journey, she made frequent stops to glance over her shoulder.

Come on, come on!, Meyer thought.

When she finally arrived at a spot directly across from him, she looked carefully to her right and to her left like a child about to cross a dangerous intersection, and then walked toward him. Meyer did not move from his position on the bench but merely raised his eyes to watch her as she approached. Her eyes, never seeming to rest in one place, darted about the area like frightened birds. She sat at the other end of his bench but didn't yet look in his direction.

Meyer looked directly at her, then he was sure of it. She was a younger version of her mother, somewhere in her late twenties, and very attractive.

She wore a long scarf wrapped once around her throat,

and her coat was open to reveal a white wool sweater that clung to her body. When she saw his eyes linger over the heavy roundness of her breasts, she closed the coat with one hand, while with the other she pushed a long strand of blond hair away from her face. When she moved her head her long, golden hair tumbled in a cascade across her shoulders.

"Herr Meyer?" Her voice was small, barely a whisper.

"Yes. You saw your mother?"

A nod. "She came to my flat. It is true, is Tony dead?"

"He's dead, killed."

Her eyes closed and her body seemed to go suddenly boneless. "Thank God, then it's over."

"You want to tell me about it?"

"Yes. I believe I have a great deal of information that will be of interest to you."

She stood and started across the park. Meyer followed her a few blocks past the exit and into a cellar café. He joined her at a table in the rear and they both ordered coffee.

Meyer tried an opening gambit. "How long have you known?"

"For about two years," she replied. "I recognized a man. I had at first seen him when I was a little girl. He was a StB, security police officer in Prague. He led a team against a group of student dissidents. I could never forget how he beat them. And then I was helping him get to the West as a Jewish refugee. It was ludicrous."

"You told Tony?"

"Yes. He said if I didn't keep my mouth shut he would turn me in and have my mother killed."

Meyer sipped his coffee and stared directly into her eyes. "Suppose you tell me the whole story."

She talked for almost an hour. Meyer digested it all and just nodded, until a name came up.

"Wait a minute. What was that name?"

"Anton. Anytime there was an emergency or a delay, I was to contact Anton. I was never given a last name."

"Where?"

"In Vienna. The number was six-oh-one-five-one-one."

"Any other special instructions?"

"Yes. I was never to give Anton my real name, only a code name, Helena."

"Why?"

"I don't know."

But Meyer knew. Polteri never wanted the left hand to know what the right hand was doing. "Did he ever mention any other names?"

"No, none."

"Vela, did you know that there is an account in your name in Vienna, a savings account with a great deal of money in it?"

To his surprise she threw back her head and laughed. She laughed so hard that tears ran down her cheeks. When she noticed that others were looking at them, she managed to get herself under control.

"He said that he was going to do that, but I thought it was only his guilt for what he tried to do with me."

Meyer leaned across the table. "What was that?"

Her face flushed slightly and her eyes wavered. "He tried to rape me."

"He raped you?" Meyer gasped, about to blurt out that Polteri was already sleeping with her mother, but managing to hold his tongue.

"No, he didn't rape me . . . but he tried. He stopped when I told him that I had never been with a man. At first he didn't believe me. Then I told him why."

Meyer cocked an eyebrow. It was hard for him to believe as well. "Why?"

"Because, Herr Meyer, I was a nun. I left the Catholic Church because of what was happening to it in my country. But I never renounced my vows."

Pieces were slowly coming together in Meyer's mind. "What happened then? I mean, what did he do?"

Vela shrugged. "He stopped pawing me. It was like he was in shock. He started crying. He said the only woman he had ever loved was a nun."

Meyer grabbed her by the arm and pulled her up. "C'mon!"

"Where are we going?"

"To Vienna. I'm taking both you and your mother over."

EIGHTEEN

She was cool, almost blasé, when she stepped through the door and saw him sitting in the pool of light from a single lamp.

"Carter?"

He gave her an easy smile and raised his glass. "Can I fix you a drink?"

"Rum with soda. And a twist of lime with lots of ice."

She shrugged out of her coat. She wore a white blouse and a long, hip-hugging black skirt very similar to what she had worn onstage.

Carter moved into the den and behind the bar. As he made the drinks, his eyes wandered up to the mirror.

He saw her hands working at a clip in her hair, then there was a jet-black shower as it cascaded down around her shoulders. She tossed it loose with a shake of her head and her hands moved to her blouse.

He turned and set her drink on the bar. "Rum, soda, lime, lots of ice."

"Thanks."

Slowly she unbuttoned the white blouse. With slow deliberateness she let it fall from her shoulders to the floor. The white half-cup bra beneath it seemed like an intrusion, out of place, a barrier to beauty. She left it on and unhooked the skirt. It fell to the floor in a puddle at her feet.

She stood sipping her drink in opaque, high-cut panties that matched the bra and accented full thighs tapering to lovely calves.

"Is that for my benefit?" Carter asked dryly.

"It was," she said, gathering the blouse and skirt. "But since it isn't having any effect, I'll get into something comfortable."

She disappeared into the bedroom and reappeared almost immediately belting a frilly peignoir around her that accented rather than hid. She took the stool beside him and tossed a leather credentials case onto the bar.

"I was wondering when you were going to get around to me."

"You weren't really that important until this afternoon." He checked the Ministry of Defence and Israeli Special Security cards, held them up to the light, and handed them back to her. "Want to see mine?"

"Not necessary. I suppose you've got everything on Polteri by now?"

"Enough," Carter said, "to know he smelled."

"He stunk." She crossed around the bar to fix her own second drink. "I'm surprised, really. When you heard about a fiancée in Rome, I thought you would come running."

"What good would it have done me?"

She shrugged. "Maybe it's better you found out about him on your own, since he was one of yours."

Carter ignored the dig. "Where do you fit in?"

She downed half the glass. "I sure as hell wasn't his fiancée."

"But you were sleeping with him?"

"Of course. I was his lay in Rome. He had 'em all over the world. Tel Aviv has had suspicions for about five years. Polteri's name popped up about three years ago. I was told to cultivate him."

"And you did."

"I did. And got enough to hang him."

Carter let his eyes stray, but only a little, never far enough not to catch the meaning in her voice as she spoke. "Why didn't you? . . . Hang him, I mean."

"The list."

Now it was his turn. He pushed his glass across the bar and she poured. "Then there *is* a list."

"Oh, yes. He told me about it himself. Do you know Porchov?"

Carter frowned. "No."

"General Maxim Porchov. He was Tony's watchdog. He was also the one who set it up from the other side, gave the word to Tony when a ringer was being put in with the real refugees. He was also Tony's paymaster."

"Ever meet him?"

She shook her head. "No, but I saw him and Tony together once, here in Rome."

"Let's get back to Tony telling you about the list."

"It was here in Rome. He said Rivkin was going to talk. He was going to run, but he wasn't worried because he had the list."

"Why would he tell you this?"

She shrugged. "I think because, in his own rotten way, he did care for me a little bit. I told him the truth, who I was, who I worked for. I told him to give us the list and Israel would give him a new identity, hide him."

"And he said . . . ?"

"He laughed and told me to go to hell."

"And the Russians got him," Carter growled.

"No, they didn't. We did."

Carter switched to plain soda. It was time to get his head clear.

"*Your* people killed Polteri?"

"Yes," she said, nodding, "but it was an accident. The whole idea was to get him off the Vienna train. He was to be brought back to Rome and then smuggled to Israel. He put up a fight and he got hit too hard."

Carter rubbed his eyes. "So there's a list, but you don't know where it is?"

"No, and obviously you don't either. I suggest we work together. If we pool information, we might find the clue."

Carter thought about this, and grinned. "I've got more access than you. I think I could get it anyway."

"Oh?" Her grin was bigger than his. "I wouldn't be too sure. Just about everything you find out, we find out soon after."

Carter bristled but he held it in check.

A tattletale in Washington? It wouldn't be the first time an Israeli spy was uncovered.

Elaine Dermott? Possible.

Hans Meyer? Maybe. He was Jewish. But . . .

"Well?" she said.

"Let me think it over, get all my ducks in a row. Will you be here in the morning?"

She moved around the bar and in between his knees. She must have applied perfume when she changed into the peignoir. The strong, musky scent filled his nostrils. She shrugged a shapely shoulder and the negligee slipped down, exposing a full breast.

"Why don't you be here in the morning?" she murmured.

"Ducks, remember? And I've got to make some calls."

"That means you're close. I'll give you another hint."

"What?"

"Tony didn't come to Rome that night to see me like he usually did."

"To drop off the list?" Carter said.

She nodded her head and shook her body. With a whisper of silk on smooth flesh, the negligee slid to the floor. She ran her hands over the curve of her stomach and up under her breasts and cupped them, forcing the dark nipples to stand out prominently while she bent her head and studied him.

"I've told you more than I should. I think it's time you reciprocated."

Her sensual body was a study of exciting contrasts: the cascade of black hair and the full red lips, the dark areolas of her swelling breasts, the narrow waist and the gentle curve of her stomach. And below it, the dark soft, tightly curled hair separating the satin cushions of her ivory-hued thighs.

"Call you first thing in the morning," Carter said, and got out of there while he still could.

"Ms. Dermott . . . ?"

"Yes?" She stopped abruptly at the marine guard's desk, her eyes searching for his name tag. "What is it, Sergeant Parker?"

"Just finishing my log from last night. I guess they couldn't get you today."

"I was out or in the communications room all day."

"Yeah, well, I got a loony call last night, and there was a name, and when there's a name, we have to check

knowledge of it with every department head, and since Mr.
Polteri—"

"Yes, yes, Parker, what is it?" she said impatiently. She
had gotten everything from Langley and the FBI. Now she
just needed to check one more thing in Polteri's personal
checkbook. She had been a fool for not bringing it with her
from the office.

"Well, the call came in from a woman. She sounded real
upset. The name was Eula Steforski—"

That was as far as the sergeant got. Elaine Dermott was
already out the door and running for her car.

Carter drove until he found a late-night café with a telephone. He dialed and a sleepy voice answered on the fifth
ring.

"Yes?"

"Sara, Nick Carter."

"Jesus Christ."

"No, Nick Carter. Sara, I need to see you."

"It's three o'clock in the morning."

"Sara, it's pressing business."

"I hate your guts. Renaldo's, near the Spanish Steps.
They're open all night."

She hung up and Carter headed for the Lancia.

Sara Geller was an Israeli. She was with an attorney
with Amnesty International in Rome. She was also a deep
cover agent for Mossad. Outside of Israel, there were
maybe six people who knew all. Carter was one of them.

Joe Crifasi had done his best, but he couldn't push the
very top-echelon private buttons that Sara Geller could
push.

Elaine slowed her car and then stopped half a block
from the Pension Prater. There were three police cars

in front of the building, their lights flashing.

As she walked forward, she slipped her credentials case from her purse.

"I'm sorry, no one behind the line."

She showed the young, uniformed officer her ID. "We got word an American was in trouble here. What's happened?"

He shook his head. "No American I know of. The housekeeper's dog raised hell in the basement while she was getting fresh cleaning supplies. They found a body in a shallow grave."

"Oh, dear. Who was it?"

"The innkeeper's wife, they tell me."

"God, how terrible. Do they know who did it? Buried her, I mean."

The young policeman shrugged. "We can't find the husband. You want me to ask about your American?"

"No, no, I'm sure it's all right."

Elaine hurried away. A few steps from her car, a man came out of the shadows and grabbed her elbow. She was about to scream and bash him at the same time, when she saw that it was Hans Meyer. "You bastard, you scared the hell out of me!" she cried.

"Sorry. What's all that about?"

She told him quickly about the phone call and what she had learned from the Austrian police officer.

"Figures," Meyer growled.

"How so?"

"I got a phone number from Vela Chebsecki. Checked it out for an address when I got back over about an hour ago. It's that building on the corner. I already paid a visit."

"And?" Elaine said.

"I found the painter . . . forger, whatever."

"Anton Robchek?"

"Yeah. His throat's been slit."

"Stefan Steforski," she said. "Very neat. And he's probably in Rome by now."

"Why Rome?"

"Because that's where Nick is. And if my information is right, that's where Polteri's list is . . . if there is one."

Quickly she explained everything she had learned so far and as much of the puzzle as she had put together.

Meyer's mind put the rest of it together from what he had learned in Budapest. "I cabbed here. C'mon, we'll take your car and call Rome from Polteri's apartment!"

Carter parked the Lancia and walked the remaining two blocks. Renaldo's was an all-night café inhabited after midnight almost entirely by locals. Between the bar and the tables, there were about a dozen men, night workers, drinking and talking in low tones.

Carter got an espresso to help him wake up, and took a table.

It was exactly five minutes later that Sara Geller entered the café. She stood for a moment glancing over the room, then apparently noticed Carter for the first time. The table next to him was vacant. As she started to move toward it, Carter gently shook his head.

She paused and turned back to the bar. She bought some telephone tokens and exited the café. Carter waited a couple of minutes and followed. He turned right toward the steps, and after a block he heard the click of her heels fall in behind him.

They walked up on the dark sidewalk and stopped in the shadow of the Egyptian obelisk at the top of the Spanish Steps. The broad, graceful steps flowed down to the boat-shaped Bernini fountain in the middle of Piazza di Spagna.

Glowing softly, dotted with church domes, the city spread before them in the moonlight.

Carter moved into the shadows and Sara Geller joined him. "This had better be important," she murmured icily.

"It is," he said. "It may be dynamite."

He slipped the file that Crifasi had given him on Isobel Rivoli into Sara's hands and explained what he wanted.

"I don't know her," Geller said, "but I know about her. She's definitely an operative. I don't think she's handled anything big, but I know she has passed some good stuff in the past."

"I want more than that," Carter growled. "I want you to push very high buttons in Tel Aviv, and do it very quietly." He went on to tell her why.

Suddenly Sara Geller was alert, her eyes slitted in concentration. "If you're right, some very big heads could roll."

"That's the idea."

Carter heard a car door slam and the sound of a man's heels on the sidewalk below. He glanced down the street and saw a short, wide figure coming in their direction. The man spat a cigarette from his mouth, and the flaming tip drew a vivid parabola against the darkness. The car he had left was a dark Mercedes. It was empty.

"Recognize that guy?"

She peeked. "No."

"I'm probably paranoid."

At the base of the steps, the man turned away from them into a doorway.

"How soon do you need all this?"

"Yesterday," Carter said.

She sighed. "It will mean getting an awful lot of people out of bed."

"It's worth it, Sara, believe me. Now go down the other

side to the Via Condotti. I'll check your back."

She slipped away and Carter eyeballed her all the way to her car. He watched until her taillights had disappeared. When he was sure no one had fallen in behind her, he moved back down the steps himself.

In front and to his left he saw the man from the Mercedes in the doorway. Carter unbuttoned his coat and slid his hand inside until his fingers were touching the Luger.

He heard the soft padding of footsteps behind him, and slowed his pace.

Two so far, he thought. Fair odds.

He was still a good four blocks from his car. If he ran, would they shoot? He doubted it.

The street was deserted. A taxi was slowly cruising the other side of the street, his way. Carter didn't want a confrontation now. If he could get to the taxi he could lose them fast and double back to the Lancia.

The footsteps behind him speeded up. At the same time, the one in front stepped out of the doorway. He was big, swarthy, definitely Italian. He held his hands far out to his sides.

"Carter, could we talk?"

The Killmaster's arm moved, but a second too late. The one in the back dropped his elbow before the Luger cleared his belt. Carter sidestepped and jammed down hard on the man's foot as he swung past.

The movement was enough to shake the Luger loose, and it clattered on the sidewalk. Before Carter could retrieve it, they both came in swinging.

Carter kicked one of them in the groin, hard. The man doubled up with a bellow. But Carter got a fast one-two in the stomach and face from the other one, and was slammed back against the brick wall. The man followed up, but Carter short-jabbed him, forcing him away.

The one Carter had kicked was back up. He saw then that the man had one arm in a sling. He used it, grabbing the broken wing and spinning him into his comrade.

The taxi had pulled up a block away, the driver settling back for a snooze. Carter ran for it. The rear door was locked. He yanked the front open.

"Move fast and you make money."

The driver's face came around, grinning, and Carter recognized him at once from the flight to Vienna: Justin Feinberg.

Carter started to back out, but he was too late. Two more of them came up on his rear from a doorway. It was a setup right from the start. The two Italians were the decoys. He guessed that Aaron Horowitz and Otto Franz were the ones behind him.

"Don't do anything foolish," Feinberg said.

Carter glanced down at the automatic six inches from his stomach and felt the prod of another gun in the small of his back.

The rear door swung open. The man behind shoved him toward it and Carter decided he couldn't argue with two guns. He bent down to get into the car and felt the bite of a hypo in his thigh. He made the seat and his vision went out of focus.

His last conscious reflection was the strong, lingering aroma of a very distinctive perfume.

NINETEEN

The buzzing of the phone barely penetrated Joe Crifasi's sleep. An awareness that it was a buzz and not a ring finally got through and he stirred. A buzz meant the private, hotline number.

He forced himself through the layers of darkness as if he were heavily drugged. One eye opened and rolled toward the clock.

Nine-thirty.

Three hours' sleep. No wonder he felt like hell.

He opened the cabinet by the bed and groped for the phone. "Yeah."

"Joe Crifasi?"

"Yeah. Who's this?"

"Elaine Dermott, in Vienna. I've been calling the number that Nick gave the embassy for hours."

"Nick's a busy man," Crifasi said, trying to support himself on one elbow. All he wanted to do was fall back against the pillow and go to sleep.

"I had to raise hell in Washington to get this number. Are you awake?"

"No," Crifasi groaned. "I wound up a big one last night, two months' work. And I'm bushed."

"Well, get unbushed," the woman barked. "I've got it."

"What have you got?"

"I think Hans Meyer and I have figured out where Polteri parked his insurance . . . the list."

"Just a minute." Crifasi staggered into the bathroom and turned on the shower, ice cold. He put his head under it for a full minute, then grabbed a towel and returned to the phone. "I'm back."

"Okay, here are the pieces. You've got to get them to Nick. Tony Polteri was married. I found out the dates, but the civil records have disappeared from the courthouse in Providence, Rhode Island. The marriage was evidently annulled."

"So what, he was married," Crifasi replied, trying to focus.

"Listen. There's a florist in Providence, Rosselli's. Four times a year for the last twenty-odd years, Tony Polteri sent a check to Rosselli to put flowers on a child's grave. You got that?"

"I got it."

"The child was Antonia Polteri. We got the mother's name from the child's birth record. Her maiden name was Joanna Santoni. I won't go into it now, but Meyer thinks Joanna Santoni may have become a nun, and there's a good chance she's in Rome."

"What makes you think that?"

"Because, of all the other quirky things Tony Polteri did, he donated almost a million dollars to the children's hospital fund of St. Maria of the Holy Martyrs."

"I know the church," Crifasi said. "It's in Trastevere."

"Have you got a connection in the Vatican?"

Crifasi paused. "I do, but I don't like to use him more than I have to."

"Believe me," Elaine replied, "this is important enough. And when you find out, get it to Nick as soon as you can."

The line went dead. Crifasi went to the other phone. He had to dial four numbers before he got his man.

"Father Dionno, it's Joe Crifasi."

"Oh dear."

"No big deal, Father, just a little favor."

The other man laughed. "They are all little favors. Did you do your Easter service?"

"I even made confession, Father."

"It's a sin to lie, Joseph, especially to a priest. What do you need?"

"Joanna Santoni. She's a nun now, maybe at St. Maria's in Trastevere."

"Is your number the same?"

"It is."

"I'll get back to you."

Crifasi shaved in the shower and then stood under ice-cold water for five minutes. By the time he was dressed and had put two cups of coffee in his belly, he thought he could cope.

He called his secretary at Amalgamated Press and Wire Service's Rome office. There were no messages from Carter. Still using the hotline phone to keep the other one open, he called the villa. No answer.

He drank more coffee and paced.

It was almost two hours later when the phone rang.

"Joseph?"

"Yes, Father?"

"Sister Gianna. She's been with the order here in Rome at St. Maria's for nearly eight years."

"Thank you, Father."

Crifasi hung up the phone and stared out the window. It had started to rain.

Now all he had to do was locate Carter.

He awakened to pain, bone-wracking, skin-burning pain. And yet there was that psychological ease that comes to one when he awakens after a serious operation and knows that he's still alive, that the worst is over.

But slowly, as the red haze lifted from his brain, Carter knew it wasn't over.

The stock question: *Where am I?*

Then he remembered. He didn't know.

He had come awake strapped to a chair in a cozy room that belonged to a farmhouse. Around him there were the two Italians and Otto Franz. The Italian with the sling on his arm had asked the questions. Carter had given them vague answers.

Then before the next questions, Otto had gone to work with his fists, expertly.

That thought brought up the next stock question: *How am I?*

He was lying on a bed. Thoughtfully, they had placed him on his side so he wouldn't choke to death on his own blood.

He moved, a little and then a little more, and then took stock.

His face was hamburger, he could feel that. The nose probably broken, and one eye puffed shut. His back, most likely the kidneys, had caught hell, and a few of his ribs were in bad shape. All four limbs seemed to be working, if he could get his motor center to make them move.

There was a table of plain dark wood next to him, and between his eyes and the table was a small area of white cloth, most of it too close to get into focus. It was hard to get even the table into focus because only his right eye was open.

He raised his left arm carefully and swung it toward the table, and the hand floated into his vision as a large, slightly blurred object that moved on and struck the table, although he did not feel it, and something clattered to the floor.

The area beyond the table grew lighter as a door opened behind him and cast its light on the far wall. Instinctively, he drew his left arm close to protect his face.

It was good old Justin Feinberg, as cute and roly-poly as he had been on the airplane and in the taxi.

"Good, you're awake."

"I—I . . ." He couldn't speak. His mouth was dry.

"Are you in any pain?"

"Yes." The word was whispered, a secret. "Could I—have—some water?" But his lips would not close over the *v* and the *m* and it sounded like a comic dialect, "hab sub water."

"Sure." Feinberg disappeared. It was not worth moving to see where he had gone. Immediately, as far as Carter knew, Feinberg was back. He held a glass to Carter's mouth, cradling his head. Even though he tipped the glass very slightly, some of the water slopped out over Carter's chin and he smiled crookedly, foolishly. "Sorry."

"No problem," Feinberg replied offhandedly.

Carter forced his voice to work. "You're so fucking solicitous. Are you really Jewish?"

The man sighed. "No, I'm East German. My comrade and I—"

"Aaron?"

"Yes. We were brought over to help as the operation grew."

"The Italians?"

"Pietro and Glenno? They are local help." His gaze turned on Carter, and it was anything but solicitous. "Look, Carter," he hissed, "we want the list. We know it exists and we know you know where it is."

"I don't."

He was ignored. "We are all in the same game. Why don't you just tell us? After all, it's *your* man who was the traitor. You give us the list without any copies being made, we don't expose Polteri. He dies a hero, and you live."

"You won't kill me," Carter said. "Too many repercussions."

Feinberg chortled. "Sadly, you're right. Well?"

"Fuck you."

Feinberg stood and moved to the door. "Otto, we start again."

The two Italians and the huge German pried Carter off the bed and half carried, half dragged him down a hallway.

This was a different room, in a basement with brick walls. Carter saw Stefan Steforski sitting behind a plain wooden table on which was an ashtray and a gooseneck lamp with an oversize reflector and powerful bulb.

The lamp was turned off. Facing the table and three feet back was a wooden stool, the only other piece of furniture in the cellar room. Steforski told Carter to sit down and got out a package of cigarettes. He didn't offer one.

"Obviously, Carter, you have a great deal of tolerance to pain."

"It's probably because I'm brain dead."

"Do you know who I am?"

"Porchov?" Carter replied.

The man nodded. "I don't want to kill you, Carter. Obviously it would cause problems, the eye-for-an-eye crap your people love so much. There are chemicals, however."

The Killmaster managed a smile through his cracked, bleeding lips. "Bullshit. If you had chemicals—and someone who could properly administer them—it would already have been done."

A sharp stinging blow under the ear cut off Carter's voice. He managed to retain his seat on the stool, and while he rubbed his neck, glanced at Otto's hand, expecting to see knuckle dusters. His knuckles were bare.

Porchov interpreted the glance correctly. "Otto has broken tougher men than you."

"Were they all sitting down?"

Otto swung again, and even though Carter was expecting it, the blow managed to knock him off the stool. He got to his knees and Otto kicked him in the stomach. Carter doubled up and Otto was about to kick him in the face when Porchov called him off. After a time, Carter crawled back onto the stool.

"He will maim you for life." Porchov's voice was completely dispassionate. "*If* he doesn't kill you. Where is the list?"

"You're stupid, Porchov. I really don't know."

"We have covered everyone," the Russian said. "The woman in Budapest, Polteri's people in Vienna, his mistress here in Rome, Rivoli. None of them has made a move. Only you, Carter, had access to Polteri's privacy."

"You're right," Carter gasped, "and it's a blank."

Porchov switched on the lamp and adjusted the gooseneck until the powerful beam was directly on Carter's face. Carter screwed up his eyes, hoping they would become accustomed to the glare, but all he could see when he opened them again was a hazy blue outline. He concentrated on thinking up a story Porchov would buy, but the permeating body odor of the gorilla standing at his shoulder was not thought-stimulating. He glanced up. The beam was adjusted to cut him off at the neck.

"You can walk out of here on your own feet. You can crawl out, or you can be carried out. It's up to you. Where is the list?"

"Vienna," Carter cracked. "The safe-deposit box."

Porchov stood, disgust on his face. "You opened that safe-deposit box two days ago. If you had found the list, you wouldn't be in Rome."

He moved to a set of stairs, light coming from the top, and stopped. The two East German phonies flanked him.

"Pietro, Glenno, keep working on him. Otto, I don't want him to die, but I want it painful."

They had barely disappeared up the stairs when Otto started in again.

It didn't take long for Carter to force himself into blackness.

Maxim Porchov tapped the table impatiently as the phone rang.

"Yes?"

"He is a fool, or he really doesn't know," Porchov said.

"Then I should go ahead?"

"Yes. He is in the cellar. The Italians and Otto will be the only ones here."

"And they are expendable."

"Of course," Porchov replied. "Crifasi?"

"He's been moving a lot. I think he has something."

"How long?" Porchov asked.

"An hour at the most, if I can convince him."

"You can, and will. We'll be ready."

Porchov dropped the phone back to its cradle and motioned the other two men to follow him as he walked from the house toward the black Mercedes.

TWENTY

Joe Crifasi paced his flat, a beer in one hand and a cigar in the other. He had done everything he could up to this point, and so far no Carter.

The Lancia he had reported to the police as stolen. He had two men, long-hair hippie types, loitering around St. Maria with orders to observe but not move. With everything else that was constantly going on in Rome, that was all the bodies he could spare, especially until he got word from Carter on a next move.

AXE was specific about that. When a field agent with an "N" designation was in your area, he was the boss. Don't move too far without his word moving you farther.

The fact that he couldn't find Carter didn't surprise him. The man had more contacts and more holes to crawl into than a Chinese puzzle.

He was about to pop another beer when his doorbell rang, making him almost jump out of his skin.

He drew the Beretta and, holding it to his side, checked the peephole. He knew her at once, the sweater exposing

183

the round smoothness of her breasts, the long dark glistening hair, and the large jet-black eyes; Isobel Rivoli.

"Yes?"

"Joseph Crifasi?"

"Who wants to know?"

"You know goddamn well who I am. Open the door."

He did, and she swept by him and turned, hands on her flared hips. "They have Carter."

"Who has Carter?" Crifasi replied, fingering the Beretta.

"Maxim Porchov. He is in a farmhouse about an hour north of Rome."

"You're sure?"

"Positive. There are three of them. I spotted them when they picked him up. I followed them, but I thought it better to get help."

Crifasi shrugged into his coat. "Are you armed?"

She smiled. "I have two Uzis and five flash grenades in the trunk of my car."

"Then what are we waiting for?"

His eyelids seemed to be glued together and it was a monumental effort to pry them apart. His mouth was so dry that he could hardly swallow.

And he was mad, as angry as he had ever been in his life, because after the last senseless beating from Otto he had realized.

There was no reason for it. Porchov had been going through the motions. He hadn't expected to get anything out of Carter. The Russian was going to find another way to the list.

And the personnel. With an operation of this size, and the value of Polteri's list, Porchov would have brought an army into play to get it.

Instead, he had two local goons who had asked questions by rote, and a beefy German whose age was probably higher than his IQ.

Porchov, Carter thought, was running scared. Why? Because Moscow didn't know that the brilliant net they had established was coming apart.

Painfully, he looked around. He was back in the same cellar room. His hands were handcuffed over a pipe leading down from the ceiling and disappearing into the furnace about ten feet in front of him.

He managed to twist his wrist around enough to check his watch. It had been almost twenty-four hours since they had picked him up. By now Crifasi would be wondering. Sara Geller would have the info he wanted and be wondering why he hadn't called.

And Meyer. Surely Hans would be back from Budapest. He and Elaine would have compared notes.

Above him, the cellar door was open. He could hear them talking while they ate.

Bastards, he thought, *taking a snack break in between bouts of beating the shit out of me!*

He propped his back against the wall and alternately thought about how he could break the pipe and tried not to think how stupid he had been.

It was then that all hell broke loose upstairs.

The rain got heavier the farther north they drove from Rome. In another hour, maybe less, dawn would break.

Joe Crifasi hunched his shoulders, his eyes intent on the road, a cigar between his teeth. The ashes dribbled down the front of his jacket with the bouncing of the car.

Beside him, Isobel Rivoli checked and rechecked the Uzis. Now and then she would look up and grunt a change of direction. That's about all the conversation that had passed between them since leaving the city.

"There, that next right, and kill your lights."

Crifasi turned, killed the lights, and idled down. "How far?"

"It's about a mile over those hills. Park under those trees."

The sound of the engine had barely died when they were both moving overland. Minutes later, they topped a small rise.

"That's it," she whispered.

The farmhouse was built with the stones from the fields surrounding it, and mortared together with cracking cement. It was set on about two acres of land, and completely surrounded by a high wall of mortared stones topped with tiles.

"How do you want to do it?" she asked.

The windows on the upper floor were shuttered. The only light was on the first floor, about midway between the front and rear.

Crifasi shrugged. "You've been here before. You call it."

"I'll take the front," she said, "you come in from the rear. What time do you have?"

"Exactly fifteen to the hour."

She nodded. "We go on the hour."

Without another word, she moved soundlessly away, to the right, and Crifasi moved to the left. He jogged along a creek, crossed on some rocks, and came up behind the wall.

He chose a section of the wall hidden under the bough of a tree and used the rocks to go up and over. The garden on the other side was overgrown and neglected. Dwarf fig and olive trees gave him good cover right up to the rear of the house.

Twenty feet from the lighted windows he crouched and checked his watch.

Three minutes to go.

But Isobel Rivoli hadn't waited.

The flash from one of the grenades blew the window out, and then Crifasi heard the chatter of her Uzi.

He sprinted forward and dived through the shattered window. He tucked, rolled, and came up on one knee. What he saw almost made him lose what dinner he had eaten.

Isobel Rivoli stood in the kitchen doorway, methodically pumping slugs from the Uzi into the three men.

The sudden silence from above gave Carter a tense moment. Then he saw Crifasi on the stairs, and right behind him Isobel Rivoli.

"Jesus, my man, they sure did a number on you," Crifasi said.

"They did that," Carter murmured, his slitted eyes studying the woman's face.

She broke first. "The keys to the handcuffs must be on one of them."

She darted back up the stairs. Crifasi started to check Carter's condition.

"Elaine Dermott called from Vienna. She thinks she's figured it out."

"The list is in Rome," Carter said.

Crifasi nodded. He started to speak, but she was coming back down the stairs.

"I've got the key."

They got Carter down from the pipe.

"You going to make it?" she asked.

"Yeah, I'll make it. Where are we?"

Crifasi told him as Carter staggered to his feet.

"Okay, let's get out of here before the neighbors get too curious."

With Crifasi's help they made it up the stairs. In the kitchen, Carter spotted his Luger and the stiletto on the table. He shoved them into his belt and followed the other two outside.

The cool night air did wonders to clear his head. As they walked the mile or so to the car, Crifasi gave Carter a rundown on the telephone call from Vienna.

Isobel walked between them. "You mean he used a nun?" she said, then snorted. "That would be just like Tony."

They were nearly to the car now. Suddenly, Carter stumbled. It was a natural reaction for the woman to throw out her arms to steady him.

Only the Killmaster didn't fall. He whirled and brought his fist up from the deck, burying it to the wrist in Isobel Rivoli's stomach.

She gasped for air and folded like an accordion. Carter chopped her on the side of the neck and she was out.

Crifasi just gaped. "You know what you're doing?"

"I don't have proof positive," Carter growled, "but as soon as we find a phone I might. If I'm wrong, she isn't hurt much. Let's get her in the car."

Sara Geller answered on the first ring.

"It's me," Carter said. "What have you got?"

"Lots. It took some digging and arm twisting, but right now two very important people in Tel Aviv are talking their heads off."

"Talk to me," Carter hissed.

"Your hunch was right. The daughter died right after the family was sent into exile."

"And this one took her place?"

"Yes. The mother stayed in line to keep her husband alive. Chances are she had the 'auto accident' when word reached Tel Aviv that her husband was dead. Jesus, Nick, they've managed to get five people in that we've learned about so far."

"Don't feel bad," Carter said. "There are a lot more all over the place."

"My friends would very much like to ask this little lady a lot of questions."

Carter smiled. "Sara, I think it's only fair that you get some reward for all your help. We're on the Milan highway about four miles out, a gas station."

"I have help," she said. "We'll be there in twenty minutes."

Carter hung up and returned to the car. Isobel Rivoli was in the back seat, like a statue, her dark eyes glaring pure hatred at him through the window.

Carter got in beside her. "It was a lot of things. They should have trained you as much as they brainwashed you. But then you were awfully young when you started, weren't you? There wasn't time for the finer points."

"I don't know what you're talking about."

"Your ass you don't," Carter said with a harsh laugh. "Good old Stefan—or should I say Porchov—did everything he could to steer me toward the 'fiancée' in Rome. Then you tell me the fiancée bit was just to get me here. You two should have gotten your stories straight. And your perfume. My God, woman, how long did you sit in that cab they used to haul me out here? You stunk it up so bad I couldn't miss it. There's a lot more, but it's not worth going into now. Did Polteri know about you?"

She shrugged. "Yes. It was a break when they assigned me to work with him to investigate the refugee smuggling ring."

"I'll bet it was," Carter hissed. "You both just fed Tel Aviv and Washington tons of disinformation. Where's Porchov?"

Silence.

Carter reached forward. He wrapped the fingers of his left hand around her throat and squeezed.

"The Israelis very much want to talk to you. You have two choices . . . talk to them and swallow a jail sentence in Haifa . . . or die, now."

There was fear in her eyes but she remained silent.

He squeezed, harder and harder. She began to gasp and claw at his arm.

"What . . . what do you want?"

"What happens to the two flunkies when you get the list?"

"Porchov will kill them. He wants no witnesses to what has happened."

"His screw-up, you mean." Carter dragged her from the car. "Come on, you're making a phone call."

It's a flat we used as a safe house when we moved them through Rome. Porchov could also meet Tony there if a meeting or payoff was needed. It's near the Coliseum.

She had said it, and then laughed.

The last time I saw Tony was in that flat.

Now Isobel was on her way to Tel Aviv and Carter was on the roof of the flat. He dropped down to an old, rusted fire escape and went to work taping the bedroom window.

Seconds later he had a windowpane taped thickly, and when a hard gust of wind hit, he rapped the glass sharply. The glass cracked and he lifted out the shattered section, carefully worked loose the rest, then stuck his hand through and unlocked the window. A moment later he stood inside the bedroom.

He went to the closed door and listened. He eased the door open and found a carpeted hallway. Light oozed through another door at the end of the hall.

Porchov stood at the window, a glass in his hand, gazing down at the street.

Carter moved silently into the room, the silenced Luger cocked. "Porchov."

The man whirled, the glass dropping from his hand when he recognized Carter.

"She won't be coming, Porchov."

The man's face was falling apart, but he managed to speak. "What do you plan for me?"

Carter shrugged. "Make a phone call, give you back to them."

Porchov nodded. "That would figure." He started toward a sideboard a few feet to his left. "There's a revolver in the top drawer..."

Carter waited until the man's fingers were tugging out the drawer before he fired.

There was a dull popping sound, and a look of sheer amazement distorted Porchov's face. His mouth opened but no cry came. He staggered back against the wall, and still gasping, his knees buckling beneath him, he fell forward.

Carter stood over him. His eyes were open and he was still breathing.

Carter moved the snout of the silencer within six inches of his forehead and fired again.

The rain had stopped. The sun was out but there was a brisk breeze blowing off the mountains.

Carter waited on a bench by the fountain. He stood

when he saw her emerge from the side door of the church.

She was radiant, very beautiful, with her full lips curled in a tiny smile.

"Mr. Carter, I am Sister Gianna. It's about Tony, isn't it?"

He reached out and took her two slender hands in his. "Yes, Sister. It's about Tony."

DON'T MISS THE NEXT NEW
NICK CARTER SPY THRILLER

ISLE OF BLOOD

Louis Corot knew Damascus well. They drove almost all the way across the city without once using a main thoroughfare. The car was clean and their papers were good, but on the main streets there was always the chance they would be stopped on a whim and questions asked.

As he drove, Corot passed on to Carter the info he had gotten on Marchand and Boudia from his Damascus contacts.

"We'll hit Marchand first," Carter said, passing his Beretta across the seat. "I'll go up, you cover my back."

Minutes later they were in one of the oldest and poorest sections of the sprawling city. Overhead lights gave way to dim streetlights set far apart. The gutters were clotted with garbage and refuse of every description. Faded, dimly lit signs announced small cafés and run-down hotels.

Corot had scarcely parked when ragged teen-agers appeared out of the shadows. He passed out warnings along with coins: if the car was not whole when they returned, he would personally molest every boy in the neighborhood.

They walked down the sidewalk to a narrow, four-story building, identical with a dozen others in the block. There was a short stoop of stone stairs, hollowed by use. The door was ajar.

Inside, there were a dozen men lounging at tables drinking glasses of tea or arak. In the rear was a counter and stairs to the next floor. All conversation ceased as they made their way to the counter and the huge black standing behind it.

"Arak," Corot said, and Carter nodded.

Two glasses of the thick, dark liquid were set in front of them, and Carter slid a twenty-pound note toward the black.

"Keep it," he said in French. "Pierre Marchand?"

"Who would like to know?"

"Two gentlemen from Tunis," Corot said, "interested in employment."

A telephone came from beneath the counter. The black spoke quietly into it, and looked up. "Do you have references?"

"Chavis, Tangier," Carter said, "Borosco in Rome. There are others." Both of the men he mentioned were notorious recruiters in their respective areas. Any idiot who would put his ass on the line for a few dollars and a holiday in the jungle had come across one if not both.

"One of you at a time. Second door on the right, upstairs."

Carter moved around the counter and the black stopped him at the foot of the stairs. The frisk was quick and efficient. When the black nodded, Carter headed up the stairs.

Behind him, he heard conversation return to the room. Out of the corner of his eye he saw Louis Corot move around to the end of the counter. From there he could see every man in the room and the big black man's hands.

Carter went up two flights of wooden stairs. The air was close and smelled of heavily spiced, overcooked foods.

He knocked, and the door was opened by a slim, dark-haired girl. She wore a stained red robe that gaped open above the belt, revealing tiny, just-budding breasts. Her skin was flawlessly smooth, the color of creamed coffee, and her eyes were dark and flashing.

From inside, a guttural growl in French. "Bring him in here, girl."

The girl studied Carter, her lips twisting into a leering smile. "Go in," she said, and moved aside a few inches.

Carter moved down a hall and into a living room of tattered furniture and heavy red drapes. Old newspapers and debris literally covered the floor.

A three-hundred-pound hulk sat at a sturdy wooden table, gorging himself. The table was laden with plates of greasy lamb, chicken, bowls of rice, and various meats wrapped in vine leaves.

"Pierre Marchand?"

The man nodded, belched, and waved Carter to a chair opposite his at the table. The Killmaster leaned forward before he sat. The hulk had a huge napkin draped across his lap. There was another just to the right of his plate, spread. It seemed to cover yet another dish of food.

"What name do you use?"

"Stassis," Carter said, moving the passport just fast enough across the other man's eyes, "for now."

A belch. "One name is as good as another." He picked something from a front tooth. "My supper. You hungry?"

Carter shook his head.

"Arak?"

Carter nodded.

"Girl."

The young girl stepped forward and poured from an earthenware jug. A smile twisted her full red lips as she handed the glass to Carter.

"Enough," Marchand growled. "Go find something to do—play with the television set."

She shrugged and sauntered from the room. Marchand stared after her, smiling at her small round hips and the backs of her brown legs.

"Nice, huh?"

"A little young," Carter replied.

"No. She's thirteen, just right. Bought her from a trader in Azziz over in Jordan." He picked up a peach from the bowl of fruit on the table and bit into it strongly, tearing a chunk free with big white teeth. "How you hear about my contract?"

Carter jiggled a hand from side to side. "On the streets. A man named Savine, Lupat Savine." He watched the slitted eyes in the folds of fat. No reaction.

"Don't know the name, but that means nothing." The peach gone, Marchand dived back into the lamb and rice. "Where you work? Who for?"

Carter rattled off places and names, and added bits and pieces of expertise such as explosives and some high-tech munitions.

"Impressive, very impressive," Marchand said, chewing away vigorously. "Almost too impressive. How come I never meet you before?"

"I never had to work this cheap before," Carter said coolly.

The room reverberated with Marchand's laughter. "I like you." Suddenly the laughter stopped. "But I don't like the shit in your mouth. You're right, though, old Pierre, the fat man, he gets the shit contracts. You don't look like the type takes a shit contract."

"It never hurts to ask," Carter said, tensing his body. "Where's the action and what's the pay?"

The man lowered his fork and looked up at Carter, still smiling slightly. But his slitted brown eyes were irritable. "I can't use you. Now, you be a good boy and take a walk."

Carter persisted. "If it's Drago Vain and Cyprus, I'm interested."

The dark eyes flashed. "I don't know who you are, smartass, but walk now before your lip gets you—"

Carter mashed the table into Marchand's belly before he got all the words out. He went over backward with a roar, and the room shook when he hit the floor. Carter yanked the napkin aside and snapped up the big Webley revolver it had hidden.

Another roar brought Marchand to his feet. He heaved his enormous bulk at Carter, who danced agilely to the side. As the hulk came past, Carter smashed him across the face with the barrel of the Webley. The impact of the blow sent Marchand across the table. Food scattered in every direction, and the big body landed on the floor in the middle of it.

Carter put his knee in the man's gut and squeezed his throat with his left hand. When the mouth opened, he put three inches of the Webley's barrel in Marchand's mouth and rattled it around.

"Listen and listen good, you fat tub of guts. I don't care any more about you than camel shit. I know you're recruiting for Drago Vain."

Blood spewed from the crease in Marchand's cheek, mixing with the lamb grease and gravy. He was breathing rapidly, his eyes flaming in his fat face.

Slowly, Carter removed most of the barrel from his mouth.

Instantly, in a high, screeching voice, he began to curse Carter, spitting out epithets in French and Arabic as if they were dirt he was trying to get off his tongue.

"That's all," Carter said softly. "Don't say anything else."

The Killmaster thumbed back the hammer on the Webley and shoved the barrel as far as he could in the rolls of fat around the man's middle.

"You're just a name on a list. You don't talk, someone will. Good-bye, asshole."

"No, no!" Marchand shrieked. "What do you want to know?"

"Who set up the contract?"

"Vain, it was Drago himself. I met him twice."

"How many men?"

"Fifty, all grunts. I get two hundred English pounds per man."

"Where do they do the time?"

"Cyprus. I deliver them in Tunis, equipped. They ship out on a freighter."

"When?" Carter hissed.

Marchand seemed to have second thoughts. His eyes began darting around the room and Carter could feel a sudden tenseness in his bulky body. He buried the Webley in fat clear to his wrist.

"Do you know how long it takes to die with a bullet in the gut, Pierre?" he growled. "Now answer my question . . . *When?*"

"Two weeks from tomorrow, the seventeenth."

"Good, very good, Marchand. One more to go. Who's the paymaster?"

"I don't know." He howled in pain as Carter put all his

weight on the knee in his gut. "I swear I don't know! It comes out of an account in Switzerland, the Credit Suisse Nationale."

Carter stood and headed for the hall.

"Hey, you . . ."

Carter turned. Marchand was on his feet, holding one hand against the angry gash in his cheek. "Yeah?"

"You'll never get out of Damascus alive. I'll come after you."

Carter walked back across the room, hefting the big Webley in his hand. "No, you won't, Pierre." His voice was soft, his smile thin-lipped. "Because if you do, I'll finish this. I'll feed five inches of this in your face and then blow the back of your head off. So you're not coming after me, Pierre. You're going to crawl into a hole until I've got Drago Vain. Because if you don't make contact now and tell him you're off the contract, he'll kill you faster than I will."

Carter turned and slammed from the room, moving quickly down the hall. The child-woman was leaning against the wall by the door. Just as Carter opened it, she came up on her toes and kissed his cheek.

He went quickly down the stairs, the Webley at his side. Corot was at the counter, a Beretta held loosely in each hand. The big black man now sat at one of the tables.

A dozen pair of eyes turned as Carter hit the bottom step. A dozen pair of eyes followed the two of them as they walked back to back to the front door.

—From ISLE OF BLOOD
A New Nick Carter Spy Thriller
From Jove in January 1990